GRANT'S WISH

GRANT'S WISH

T. S. Pollard

Grant's Wish
Copyright © 2020 by T. S. Pollard

First Publication 2010

Library of Congress Control Number: 2020903279
ISBN-13:   Paperback: 978-1-64749-061-4
            epub :   978-1-64749-068-3

Mystery Action & Adventure | Suspense Thrillers

All rights reserved. No part of this publication may be reproduced, distributed, or transmitted in any form or by any means, including photocopying, recording, or other electronic or mechanical methods, without the prior written permission of the publisher or author, except in the case of brief quotations embodied in critical reviews and certain other noncommercial uses permitted by copyright law.

Although every precaution has been taken to verify the accuracy of the information contained herein, the author and publisher assume no responsibility for any errors or omissions. No liability is assumed for damages that may result from the use of information contained within.

Printed in the United States of America

GoToPublish LLC
1-888-337-1724
www.gotopublish.com
info@gotopublish.com

Contents

Chapter 1 1
Chapter 2 4
Chapter 3 8
Chapter 4 10
Chapter 5 13
Chapter 6 17
Chapter 7 19
Chapter 8 23
Chapter 9 25
Chapter 10 29
Chapter 11 34
Chapter 12 36
Chapter 13 38
Chapter 14 42
Chapter 15 45
Chapter 16 48
Chapter 17 52
Chapter 18 56
Chapter 19 58
Chapter 20 62
Chapter 21 68
Chapter 22 70
Chapter 23 72
Chapter 24 74
Chapter 25 79
Chapter 26 83
Chapter 27 85
Chapter 28 90
Chapter 29 93
Chapter 30 97

Chapter 31	102
Chapter 32	106
Chapter 33	110
Chapter 34	113
Chapter 35	115
Chapter 36	119
Chapter 37	121
Chapter 38	126
Chapter 39	129
Chapter 40	131
Chapter 41	136
Chapter 42	140
Chapter 43	144
Chapter 44	147
Chapter 45	151
Chapter 46	154
Chapter 47	158
Chapter 48	161
Chapter 49	164
Chapter 50	168
Chapter 51	171
Chapter 52	175
Chapter 53	179
Chapter 54	182
Chapter 55	185
Chapter 56	189
Chapter 57	191
Chapter 58	195
Epilogue	199

A tip of the hat to Sam Ashworth,

Judy Thorn and Beth Callahan

for their help in completing Grant's Wish.

The young Indian boy was playing with other boys near his tribe's encampment, by the banks of a stream. He spotted an injured eagle on the ground, flapping its wings but unable to fly. He felt sorry for it, even though he and his young friends had sometimes shot at eagles with their arrows. They never told anyone at home about this, knowing eagles were highly regarded by the tribe.

The boy picked up the struggling bird, took it to his home, and nursed it back to health. One day the bird began to strut about in the cage, which the boy had woven from marsh reeds, so the boy released it and let it fly away. The bird rose into the sky, leaving a long gray-and-white feather on the ground. Most of the tribe watched as the bird ascended, and a very young girl picked up the feather and presented it to the boy. From then on, the boy was called "He of the Long Feather." It was a name he learned to be proud of as he grew into adulthood, though his Native American tribal members often just called him "Long Feather."

Chapter 1

Expected Letdown

On any other morning Lee Nieman would leap out of his car with enthusiasm, jump to the pavement, and walk at a fast clip to his office or wherever else he might be headed. If nothing else in his twenty-some years in the hotel business, he was known for his self-confidence and energy, on and off the job. His apartment was only a few blocks from the posh Grande Arms he managed, and he was a familiar figure to downtown Atlanta office workers, who often saw him jogging to work in his blue Nikes.

But this was certainly not his usual day. He wasn't in Atlanta. He was in Plainview, Indiana, and he had just driven hundreds of miles overnight to get there. And worse, from his standpoint, he really didn't want to be there at all—or any place in Indiana. He wasn't a happy forty-seven-year-old traveler.

He ran his fingers through a head of thick hair, which used to be black but was now pewter gray, his ex-wife called it, about the same shade of gray as the dull-finish '88 Mercedes he'd just driven. Chalk up another legal win for the ex-wife—she was probably driving to her job in the convertible that went to her in the divorce.

Nieman rolled down the window and sat there, grimacing inside at what he saw. The Silver Swan Inn was one property the Swinton Hotel Corporation didn't feature in its glossy brochures. He'd been told the historic Swan was showing its age. This was quite an understatement, he thought, looking at it. He tried to imagine what it had looked like in its glory days, but all he could see was an establishment on the downhill, not unlike his career now, after his demotion and being shunted unceremoniously to the middle of nowhere.

Slamming the car door shut behind him, Nieman stepped out to the sidewalk. Hands on hips, he leaned against a fender showing some rust and gazed at the four floors of the cranberry red Swan building. A white gazebo stood next to a rock-walled goldfish pond on a sprawling lawn shaded by a towering oak and cottonwood trees beginning to lose their yellowing leaves to the late summer season. Nearby, a small, wiry man in bib overalls was busy hauling a blower around herding just-mown grass and scattered leaves off the walking path around the hotel's broad lawn.

With an antiques shop and ice cream parlor across the street, neither open for the day, and a yelping dog chasing a squirrel across the sidewalk, the scene could have been a Norman Rockwell painting—except for the unkempt Swan itself. Nieman didn't know whether he felt sorrier for the old building or himself for being here. He stared at the century-and-a-half-old hotel and stroked his chin. It was one of the nervous habits he'd picked up after quitting his two-packs-a-day smoking routine the previous year.

The eaves and roof line of the building sagged like an old woman's hemline and the downspouts were loose, some swinging in the morning breeze. The mortar in some of the brickwork on the four-story fireplace chimney appeared to be crumbling. A small second-floor balcony looked like it might collapse at any moment. Parts of the wrought iron filigree balcony railing drooped, and green shutters on some windows dangled from their brackets.

The place looked to Nieman like a worn antique, apparently never deemed worthy of restoration. He wondered how many would-be guests had taken one look and decided to seek other accommodations that were classier and without ghosts. Nieman's colleagues back at the home office kidded him about the Swan's alleged young female ghost, who'd been seen several times over the years. They joked that she might enjoy "haunting" the just-divorced new Swan manager.

As he stood staring at the Swan, Nieman no longer wondered why it seldom turned a profit. He would have liked to talk with his predecessor, but the man had already left town, after quitting without notice.

Nieman rubbed his eyes to make sure this wasn't just a bad dream. Most of all he wanted a cigarette, but he reached in his pocket for one of the lemon drops he'd brought along for the trip, another habit he'd picked up after quitting smoking.

Chapter 2

Low-Key Welcome

The new Swan manager strode slowly toward the steps leading up to the veranda and the inn's front entrance. This was one job he wasn't in a hurry to start. From behind he heard an Appalachian-tinged voice: "Sir, excuse me, b-but would you be from the b-building inspection department?"

Startled, Nieman turned to find himself face to face with the slight-framed workman in bib overalls he'd seen earlier with the grass blower. "Why, no, I'm not," said Nieman. "You a Swan employee?"

"Sure am, yes, sir, yes, sir." The man smiled. "The name's Boney Pieratt, maintenance man. We b-been waitin' for an inspector from the city, and I thought you might be him. I'm sorry to b-bother you."

"No bother, but I'm not from the city. I'm just coming to the hotel here. My name is Nieman, Lee Nieman, and you say yours is Boney?" Nieman extended his hand to Pieratt, judging him to be about as short and scrawny a man as he'd ever met, and also as jumpy.

"We'll be working together," said Nieman with as big a smile as he could muster. "I'm here as the new manager. I understand your boss Mr. Cole left town."

"Yes, sir, yes, sir, I guess he did. He was a good man, but he up and quit a few days ago. Don't know why, but we was told you wouldn't be coming in till tomorrow." Pieratt was almost dancing on the pavement with nervousness.

"Well, I got started sooner than I expected," replied Nieman, without saying he'd left sooner because he just wanted to be gone after being officially demoted by the front office and before running into too many colleagues who'd want the details.

"You want me to t-tell Curly you're here? He's working the front desk right now—been here all night—and he's gonna be real surprised to see you right now."

"Curly?"

"It's Handley. Charles is the first name. We just call him Curly because he don't have no hair." He giggled. "You know, he's our night auditor."

"Oh sure, I should've known. But don't bother telling him now. I'll just introduce myself. You just go ahead and finish what you were doing. By the way," said Nieman as he moved away, "why was the building inspector coming here?"

"The city says that fire escape on one side ain't safe no more. Some of the wall brackets are busted off." He turned the blower on again and moved across the lawn while Nieman headed to the front door of Southern Indiana's once most famous hospitality spot.

The wooden entrance door was tall and framed by deeply fluted, carved molding, probably hand-crafted many decades ago, Nieman thought. The brass plate holding the door handle reminded him for a moment of the brass plates on the doors to the lobby of the Grande Arms he'd managed. His housekeeping crew kept the brass polished to a mirror finish, so guests could see their reflections in metal as they opened the door.

But here the only things he could see in the brass were scratches in a dull, corroded surface. The once-handsome frame around the door showed small dents and cuts in the wood. Someone had carved a heart in the wood with the initials of two long-ago lovers. On the lower panel of the door a discolored metal plaque offered a history lesson: "The Silver Swan Inn, founded by Ira Norton in 1838, was originally a stagecoach stopover for travelers going to and coming from Louisville, Indianapolis, and Cincinnati."

Nieman grabbed the door latch and stepped into the lobby, wondering if the inside of his new place of employment would be as worn as the outside. Walking to the front desk, he almost tripped on a torn area of the carpeting. He joked to himself that the carpet looked like it'd been installed about the time of the Civil War and hadn't been replaced or cleaned since. Stains and tears were everywhere. A deep breath told him the atmosphere in the lobby likely hadn't changed much either. He caught hints of 150 years of cigar and cigarette smoke infused with Lysol.

Nieman glanced around the lobby but saw no one, even at the front desk. He had to remind himself this was no city hotel with a city clientele going in and out at all hours. The Swan had only 24 rooms, not the 124 the Grande Arms had.

No one appeared at the front desk or any place else in the lobby, but he could hear country music from somewhere in the building. At least someone was alive in there.

He scanned a lobby crowded with what he guessed were genuine antiques, upholstered chairs, an aging couch, a roll-top desk, a writing table, kerosene lamps, and nineteenth-century artwork displayed on the walls. A very old butter churn occupied one corner, and in another stood a life-sized wooden Indian with a handful of cigars. Next to it stood a small, red whiskey keg with loose staves held together with iron bands. The whole lobby looked like a badly organized antique flea market crowded around an immense brick fireplace.

Nieman tried to imagine a bustling lobby of the past, with well-dressed visitors chatting and socializing in Victorian surroundings after enjoying a dinner of blackened ocean bass and fine French wines. But it was not that way today and probably hadn't been in recent decades.

From a back room, probably the bar, he could still hear country music—likely being played on an old juke box, he guessed. Nieman drummed his fingers on the front desk counter and then leaned over the counter and shouted, "Hello. Anyone here?"

Slowly, the squashy face of a balding man in horn-rimmed glasses and wearing an off-center tie with a pink shirt far too tight for his bulging stomach eased into view behind the counter. He rubbed two drooping eyes and mumbled in what Nieman suspected was a British accent: "Good evening, good evening, sir. Ha. I was just on the telephone and didn't see you there. How can we help you?"

Nieman had already been told to expect the red nose of the hotel's night auditor Curly Handley, who drank too much. He extended his hand.

"Glad to meet you, Mr. Handley. I'm Lee Nieman from Atlanta. I think you've been told I'd be here." A wide-eyed Handley stared straight ahead at him, speechless.

It doesn't get worse than this, thought Nieman. Get demoted, divorced, wind up in a place as old as the Tower of London, with a ghost, and find an employee with a hangover sleeping on the job. This place could use a good ghost—even better if she carried a feather duster and vacuum cleaner. And he was there to shut it all down. Somewhere inside he felt a twinge of guilt he couldn't explain, and he reached into a pocket for another lemon drop. It was time to update his resume.

Chapter 3

Fame in a Name

"Hello, Mr. Mayor. Nice to hear from you." Plainview's city manager, Roy Acum, had answered the phone in his office but wasn't happy the caller was the town's most talkative resident, if not its most blustery. Acum was busy at city hall, working on budgets, and didn't have time for insurance agent Charles Kash Gomia, but he could hardly ignore the call since Gomia was also Plainview's current mayor and recently became the new president of the local Rotary.

"Roy," Gomia said as Acum put down the double-entry spreadsheet he'd been studying and resigned himself to a long conversation, "I'm just checking in to see if you've talked to the state yet on the city name change?"

"Well, Charles, I've verified the procedure is like I told you. City council just has to approve it, and then if all the paperwork's in order, the state puts the final stamp of approval on it."

"That's great, Roy. You think it'll only take a few weeks?"

"I think so."

"Good 'cause most everybody's in favor of it, and it'll help keep us on the map—especially if the rumors about the Swan closing are true. I'm sure hoping they aren't."

"Well, Kash, that may be why they just sent in a new man to take over. You know, that manager they had just up and quit, so it sounds like bad news to me. The place hasn't made money in years."

"But we need it. It's the only thing in town that attracts some visitors. Come to think of it, I best got to get over there and meet the new man—name of Nieman, I think. I'd like to see what they're planning to do."

"Good idea."

"I'll ask him what the company thinks about changing our town's name. I'd believe they'd like that. More recognition value for travelers, don't you think?" Gomia said.

"Well, I—"

"Oh, I think it'll do wonders for our visibility, especially now that they've built that new highway to the interstate. I mean you have to face changes in life—right, Roy? Hell, if I hadn't faced up to all the changes in the business world, why, I guess I'd still be pickin' cotton down on the farm."

"Well, yes, I suppose so," said Acum, trying his best to end the conversation. "I've got some budgets to work on, so I'll get back with you when I hear from the state. Nice talking to you, Kash. See you la—"

Before Acum could hang up, Gomia said, "Maybe we could give them some kind of tax break that'd keep 'em in business."

"That possible."

"Just keep me posted on the name change, Roy. Oh, and say hello to your beautiful wife for me."

"Right. Bye for now, Mr. Mayor." This time Acum didn't wait to hear any last thoughts from Plainview's mayor before hanging up.

Chapter 4

A Look Around

The new Swan manager had scheduled his first employee meeting at 9:00 a.m. but had come to his office an hour earlier to start exploring his new workplace. Wandering down the second-floor hallway and turning a corner, he almost walked into a hip-high mahogany cabinet he judged to be an old console record player. But it wasn't. He lifted the highly polished lid to see a foot-wide perforated brass disk where a record might have been and realized the cabinet was an antique music box, the kind only the well-off could afford years ago. He was tempted to turn the crank on the side but opted instead to continue down the hall to the Harriet Beecher Stow Room.

Nieman found himself recalling the words of his boss, Robert Prestik, about the hotel's past glories:

> Years ago, the now-shabby property was a landmark in this part of Indiana. It boasted a proud list of dignitaries as guests and often served as the venue for numerous public events, some with national significance.
>
> When William Jennings Bryan was running for president, he gave a famous speech from the second-floor balcony to a crowd in the street. William Henry Harrison announced his

candidacy for president at a Swan banquet in the early 1800s. Even some standing presidents, including Lincoln, and US senators and state governors were overnight guests. World-famous singer Jenny Lind, on tour of the United States, came here as many others had simply to enjoy the best French menu this side of Chicago. Imported wines were amply stocked by the inn's Norton family owners. Even Ulysses S. Grant was an occasional Swan guest during the Civil War.

The names of the famous guests were still posted on the doors of the rooms they'd occupied. "Some of the original beds are still in use in those guest rooms," his boss had told him. Nieman had quipped that he just hoped someone had changed the sheets and mattresses a few times since then.

The author of *Uncle Tom's Cabin* was "an overnight guest in 1860 during a lecture tour," read a plaque by a door. Like other rooms Nieman seen, a four-poster bed occupied most of the space, with an ornate ceramic water pitcher and basin on a bedside table.

Nieman walked on, noticing artwork on the walls. One was a still life of books, a flute, and sheet music he recognized as that of a well-known late nineteenth-century American artist. He remembered once seeing a print of the same art somewhere, but this was no print. He could see brushstrokes. It was the original? He pondered that for a moment and walked on.

At the James Whitcomb Riley Room a wood-framed legend read, "Indiana's famous poet was a frequent guest at the Swan around the turn of the century." A long-ago seamstress had added embroidered lines from his poem "Our Hired Girl":

Clear out'o the way
They's time for work
An' time for play.PK as is
Take yer dough an' run child run
Er' I can't get no cookin' done.

Nieman smiled with nostalgia and walked on toward the U. S. Grant Room when his pager buzzed. He'd asked the front-desk clerk to call him when the staff began arriving for the meeting downstairs. He'd finish his tour when he had more time.

Chapter 5

Where'd the Boss Go?

Balancing a full cup of coffee in a mug displaying a Grande Arms logo, Nieman grabbed hands with everyone who'd come to his first staff gathering. He told everyone good morning and pointed to the coffee urn and a big box of Krispy Kremes he'd ordered.

He tossed a notepad on a table and sat in one of the folding chairs he'd set up for the session in the Lincoln Hospitality Room. On the wall was the local Rotary Club's big gearwheel symbol. Curly had told him Rotary was one of the few local groups still using the hotel for weekly luncheon meetings. Below that a small yellowing poster had been thumbtacked to the wall. It said, "Lions. Big fish fry Saturday. Community Park. All you can eat for $5."

As he waited, Nieman couldn't help but think of what Swinton's CEO, Stuart Tompkins, had told him after demoting and reassigning him: "Remember local politics isn't your job, and going to Indiana won't be the end of the world. You do what we're looking for there, and we'll get you back here when there's a vacancy. Just help us unload the property, one way or the other."

The CEO had told Nieman he'd been posted there "just to get it fixed up a little" before it went on the market, as well as to see if he could find the quirk in the Swan's property deed that had cropped up when Swinton bought it in a package deal with other properties a few years ago.

Nieman would do whatever he was told to do right now, or at least until he could find a new job. He knew he wasn't going to let himself get stuck long in this Hoosier backwater, picturesque as it was or as historic as the Swan might be.

The chatty buzz in the room died down as Nieman finished his pecan roll and looked around, sensing a nervous quiet in the room. He dinged his cup with a spoon, stood up, and said, "I think I've met everyone here by now, so I guess we can get right down to why I called this session, which won't last too long. I like short meetings—better yet, no meetings at all." He grinned and everyone in the room nodded approval.

"Right now there's one thing I'd really like to know. Where did your former boss Mr. Cole go? I'd like to talk to him and ask him why he quit so suddenly." Nieman searched the faces of the Swan employees for an answer. All he got was hints of smiles and a snicker or two.

"Okay, okay," he said, assuming the humor must have come from something humorous someone said. "Let me in on the joke."

"It wasn't no joke, ah, Mr. Nieman," his maintenance man said with a cheery grin. "See, we just made a bet that your first question would be about the ghost. Everybody new always asks about that."

Nieman chuckled, and everyone joined him with a round of laughs. "No. I probably would have asked that in time, but I'm more interested now in where Mike Cole went." He sipped his coffee and looked around. Except for the tinkle of cups and stirring spoons, there was silence and a few worried looks. Nieman guessed that rumors of a closing were probably all over town since Cole's unannounced departure as manager.

"Look, first, let me tell you that no one is losing his or her job right now, but we're all going to have to work hard to freshen up the place to attract more business." He felt guilty for the slight lie, since the place was likely going to be sold or torn down. The atmosphere in the room relaxed a bit. "So, if you hear anything about him please let me know. Now, any questions I can address?"

A hand shot up. "We heard that the Swan might be torn down and we'll all be out of jobs," said one of the housemaids.

"No, not anytime soon." He'd lied again; he hoped it didn't show. He was just happy no one pressed him further on the question. "Anything else?"

"Are there gonna be any changes?" asked Pieratt as he scooted his chair back and took a last drag on his hand-rolled cigarette.

"Not many," said Nieman, without telling Boney that among changes coming would be the posting of No Smoking signs in the common areas.

The food service manager moved in her chair. Nieman knew she was probably worried about her operation. He already knew from a walk through the kitchen that she had reason to worry. But, what the hell, the kitchen wasn't in any worse shape than the rest of this hotel. Nieman wasn't planning to axe her or anyone else, at least not now. He'd always had a way with people that brought the best out of them. He knew he would need that to make the place marketable and save what was left of his career.

Suddenly heads turned to the rear of the room as the door to the lobby opened and the Swan's part-time janitor walked in, apologizing for being late. "The fire chief caught me outside and asked about that railing on the fire escape," he said. "It's rusting through and hanging down to the ground."

Nieman looked around the room. "What's been the problem with getting it fixed?" He looked at Pieratt.

He responded sheepishly. "Ah, er, yes, sir, I been workin' on it but ... but it needs some welding, and I can't do no welding jobs."

"Well," said Nieman, "there'll be a bit more budget now, so we can pay for things like that." He turned to his night auditor. "But, speaking of money, ah, Curly, what's the occupancy rate been like in the past year?" He found it difficult to call the bald Brit by his Swan nickname.

Handley wiped his brow with his handkerchief and nervously scratched his ear, saying, "Ahem, well, It's been only about 30 percent lately, sir."

"You don't have to call me 'sir,' Curly," said Nieman. "It's Lee around here. But, go ahead. Does the rate ever get better?"

"Not often," replied the night auditor almost in a whisper, stroking the Windsor knot in his tie.

"That's a problem," said Nieman. "But right now we all just have to work together to get the place in shape. Anymore questions?"

The head housekeeper spoke up. "When are we going to get new sheets? The ones we have are pitiful—so old and thin you could read *Uncle Tom's Cabin* through them like a window pane." Everyone chuckled as the door to the lobby opened again.

Chapter 6

Ghost Believers

The front-desk clerk, a part-time college student, peeked in and gestured to Nieman. "Ah, sir, there's a lady here, a Miss Landrew. Says she'd like to talk to you. I told her you were busy, but she said she was busy too ... very busy."

"Who is she?" Nieman asked.

"She's a local solicitor, sir," Handley said. "She pops in all the time to talk to Mr. Cole. I mean, she did. I dislike saying it, sir, but it's usually something about someone suing the hotel. If you don't mind my saying, she's a bit of a snippy twit. Divorced ... I believe."

"Oh crap," said Nieman, slapping his hand on the table. "That's all I need is another lawyer in my life." He thought about his wife's lawyer back in Atlanta, always telling his attorney he'd have to concede another expense to satisfy his ex in finalizing their divorce.

"Tell her I'll be right out. Go ahead, people, and finish your coffee and doughnuts. We'll have another go at it later, after I've explored this crusty old place more."

He stood and added, "By the way, I really would like to know about the ghost." He stopped for a moment and grinned. "How many of you believe there really is one here?"

All hands shot up.

"I'll be damned," he muttered as he left the room, laughing but wondering what other surprises the fates might have in store for the Silver Swan's new head man.

If nothing else, he had to admit the job was getting more interesting every day. In regional TV commercials, the Grande Arms touted its indoor swimming pool, five-star dining menu, and tennis courts on the penthouse level. But no ad copywriter was ever asked to dream up twenty-second spots featuring a ghost haunting the posh suites of his former venue.

Chapter 7

Attorney in a Hurry

Missy Landrew was Plainview's only female attorney. Only a few years out of law school, she had humbled more than a few male lawyers, who had faced her in court on civil matters. Her diminutive stature hadn't proved a problem in settling personal damage disputes, especially against businesses. Opposing attorneys learned to look on her as taller and more intimidating than her five feet and two inches appeared in civil court. More often than not, she left courtrooms with a Cheshire cat grin, having demolished adversaries' arguments. More than a few file clerks had walked out of court rich for life.

Nieman had been told the Swan had attracted more than its share of minor personal damage suits. He didn't wonder why, considering the condition of the place. As he stepped into the lobby from the stairs, he found Landrew at his office door in tennis togs, jogging in place, her copper-tinged ponytail bouncing up and down through the back of a White Sox ball cap.

"Well, I guess we haven't met," he said, barely managing to keep his gaze off the trim body as it continued to run in place. "I'm Lee Nieman, and you would be …?"

"I would be Missy Landrew, attorney; my office is down the street. I'm here to tell you we have a settlement agreement from Mrs. Coolridge on the carpet thing." As she talked she pulled her earphones from her head but kept running in place.

"I have to confess, I don't know anything about that 'carpet thing' or, ah, Mrs. Coolridge was it?" he replied in as courteous a manner as he could muster. "But I'll be glad to hear all about both. Ah … are you really in this much of a hurry?" He wondered if she was ever going to stop bouncing up and down.

"I'm always in a hurry when it comes to business, Mr. Nieman. You probably think because we are here in this small town we're all in the slow lane. Wrong. I have to stay in the fast lane, or these local legal eagles would get all the business, if you catch my drift. They have the only legal fraternity here, and I'm a one-woman sorority."

"I understand, Miss … is it Landrew?"

She nodded.

"Can I get you a cup of coffee?" he said, sitting down in his office chair, which creaked as he sat.

"Not now. Got to run," she said, placing some legal documents on his desk. "This will give you the details, but just to catch you up, last spring Mrs. Helen Coolridge tripped on the carpet—that well-worn carpet with tears in it on the second floor. She hit the floor and broke her arm, a simple fracture, but she suffered considerable mental distress, as you might guess, in the process. Won't cost your company too much. I'm sure you have coverage. But she does want something a little different before she signs."

He smiled cordially and said, "Different than money?"

"Well, kind of. She wants a free room here during the county fair season."

"Why? Doesn't she live in town?"

"Yes, but it'd be for her former husband. He farms and comes here for the fair every year. She doesn't want him to stay with her when he's in town. They get along now, but she wants to make sure he doesn't come too close to her. Says all he wants is sex and then he's gone again."

"Well, my, my, that's a first." He couldn't restrain a snicker as she shrugged in a what-can-I-say manner. "I'll look it over and send it on to Atlanta." Still chuckling, he asked, "Do you jog everywhere you go?"

"No, I'm on my morning run. Do about two miles a day. Good for the figure, you know. That's why I have to go now. But I think I'll be seeing you around anyway. This place is great for business," she said and then smirked.

"I'll bet. In other words, Miss Landrew, you don't chase ambulances. You just bring a legal pad over here during busy periods and fill up your appointment book?"

"The legal possibilities are endless here, as are the antiques, Mr. Nieman. Did your predecessor tell you about the woman who backed into one of those steam radiators a couple of years ago? She settled for about $5,000. Very unsafe place—I mean you don't get to be over a century old without problems."

"No, he didn't tell me anything. I haven't seen him since I got here. He split, and I don't know where he is."

"Of course he's gone. Nobody could make money on this property, not even the great Swinton chain. He did his best, I think. He certainly put in a lot of hours trying to make it work." She went on. "I don't know where he went either, but we all know why you're here, Mr. Nieman: to tear down the Swan and get rid of it. Got to be a drag on the books, right? This place probably hasn't turned a profit since Abe Lincoln stayed here. I should tell you, there're a lot of people here who wouldn't want it to disappear."

"Well, you aren't exactly on target, Miss Landrew. But we can talk about this sometime, if you'd like. I am new here, you understand. There are a lot of things I don't know about this place or about the town."

"Oh, yes, I understand," she said, raising her eyebrows and smiling in mock skepticism. She pivoted to leave, still running in place. "But I might take a rain check on the coffee ... might. Unlike your hotel, I'm always very busy."

She turned her head to give him a momentary wave and what he thought was a hint of a genuine grin as she bounced over the ancient wood floor of the front lobby to the door. He noticed she took a wide detour through the lobby to avoid the carpeted area.

Nieman suddenly realized he had missed his chance to tell her he was a regular jogger too. He usually listened to classical music tapes when he jogged. He wondered what kind of music she listened to. Through the front window of the lobby, he watched the town's only female attorney drive away in a yellow convertible.

"Hey, Boney," he yelled through the door of the banquet room after she left. "After I have a chat with Curly, how about giving me a tour of this place? I need a little history lesson. That might be about all I'll get out of this job, and maybe seeing my first ghost." He headed to his office for a sit-down with his night auditor.

Chapter 8

Sloppy Bookkeeping

The sweat was already breaking out on Curly Handley's nearly bald pate as he handed over the past month's hand-kept ledger to Nieman, while they sat facing each other in his small office. "Sir, I've kept all the books with meticulous care. I do hope you understand that."

"I do, I do. Calm down, my man. I detect a bit of British skittishness, but you don't have to worry. I've looked over the monthly work sheets your former boss sent to the home office, and I don't see any problem ... except this place doesn't do enough business and never makes any money."

"Indeed. I'm afraid you're quite right on that, sir—ah, Lee."

"I did notice one thing I thought was a bit odd," said Nieman, leafing through the ledger pages. "Except for one month early in the spring—probably during the county fair—the place made no profit all year until last month, when my predecessor left. You have any idea why?"

"No, but I noticed the same thing, and we didn't have an exceptional number of overnight guests that month either."

"Well, nobody ever argues with profit. So, let's just put it down to a numerical error in our favor."

"He wasn't very comfortable with details."

"I guess not. Anyway, my man, do you have any questions, or suggestions as to how we can drum up more business?"

"Speaking of Mr. Cole, sir, I might say he had some wonderful ideas along that line. He wanted to revive some things from the old days, like bringing Santa in during the Christmas season, staging wine tastings, and asking the high school band to play sometimes on the lawn."

"Yes, good ideas. I think we should consider doing some of those very things in the next few months. You know, Charles, I think this place still has potential."

"Oh, I do agree, sir, and I'm willing to help you pursue that potential, if you'll have me."

"Of course I would. I'm just unsure what's going to happen with the property, and frankly, I'm a bit unsure how I'll fit into the Swan's future."

"I understand, sir."

Handley left, and as Nieman moved the chair Handley had used away from his desk, he noticed a Post-It note stuck to the old chair's scooped back. Penciled letters had been scribbled on the note: "C h a N T V V s S f i N v."

"Probably a forgotten reminder." Nieman mused, pulling it off and sticking it on the front of a drawer in his desk. He leaned back in his swivel chair, gripped his hands behind his head, and gazed at a once-white ceiling now yellowed with decades of cigarette and cigar smoke. He pondered the note, wondering what it might have meant, if anything—just another mystery in a place brimming with mysteries.

CHAPTER 9

Penny for a Wish

Nieman and his scrawny maintenance man headed toward the rear of the Swan grounds, where a two-floor carriage house stood, covered in vines and mostly vacant. Behind a half-opened door on the ground floor stood an old Nash Rambler convertible rusting away in what likely was once garage space for hotel vehicles. To Nieman it had the smell of an old barn. "What's that all about, Boney?"

"Well, I don't rightly know. Guess a long time ago they used to keep horses in there for people staying overnight. The upstairs was fixed up a long time to live in. That's where the boss stayed."

"Sounds like a good place for me too, if we can get it cleaned up a little. It'll get me away from that music in the bar I can hear in my room. I'm not into country music."

The two turned to walk to the other side of the building.

"How long have you worked here, Boney?" asked Nieman as they ambled toward a tall sycamore tree that shaded the rock-walled goldfish pond.

"I've been working here about fi-five years now," said a nervous Pieratt. "Mr. Nieman, are you gonna lay me off? I know

I ain't no great maintenance man. I can fix cars pretty good, but I don't know much about fixin' toilets and plumbin,' and I can't weld or I'd be fixin' that second-floor fire escape."

"Don't worry. I'm not cutting anybody back right now."

"Well, sir, I was afeared I didn't make a very good impression first time we met outside last week, scattering grass and leafs all over you."

"No. I didn't even think about it. But tell me about yourself and how you got hired in the first place."

"I met Mr. Cole at a Vietnam vets meeting one evening, when his car wouldn't start. I helped get it going for him. Then we jes' started talking about the hotel and how he was getting more money from the company for some remodeling. Said he'd get me trained on welding and dry walling, so I could help him do some of the work." Pieratt talked as the two sat on the rock wall of the goldfish pond. "But I stuck around just to do the regular maintenance, like fixin' blown fuses and painting, that kinda thing. This place ki-kind of sticks to you, if you know what I mean. My daddy used to say a job is like getting married. If you love your woman and she loves you back, life'll be beautiful. But if you don't love your wife or she don't love you, you might as well be in prison."

"Sounds right to me," said Nieman, looking down at the pond and thinking about when his marriage went off the tracks. "I imagine this is the pond I've heard about, where the school kids throw in pennies and make a wish?"

"Yes, sir, this is what they ca-call Grant's Wishing Pond. Kind of famous around here. Bottom's filled with pennies. It's a tradition, you might call it. They just say, 'Please grant my wish'—have to use say 'grant' a'course—and toss in their pennies. The local schools use the pool like a history lesson, tell'n the kids about the general and the Civil War. General Grant's a big name round here. Fact is there's a move on to change the town name to Grantville, yes, sir. Speaking of the general, that room on the second floor, where he always stayed, is where some people has seen the ghost they talk about."

"Hmmm," muttered Nieman, scratching his chin and reaching in a pocket for a lemon drop. "Have you ever seen the ghost?"

"No, sir," said Pieratt, "and don't want to neither, but a couple of people who stayed here overnight a few years ago told me and the boss about seeing the ghost. Never believed it myself, but you know, where I come from in Kentucky lots of people claim they seen ghosts, like dead relatives, in the old silver mines."

Nieman nodded and pointed at the Swan building. "Look at the back of the building, the brick part. I noticed when I first got here the whole back end of the building looks like it's settled down a little."

"Yes, sir, sure has. I guess that happened over all them years. Probably 'cause the ground sunk beneath it. People around town say there was passageways dug out underneath the hotel a long time ago to hide slaves in while they was escaping to the North. Called it the Underground Railroad." He paused a moment to roll a cigarette from his sack of Bugler tobacco. "They say that caused the ground to sink a little under the foundation. I don't know if there's really any tunnels. I never look around too much in the cellar. It's a dirty, nasty place."

The two got up and walked through a yard scattered with saucer-sized, yellowed tree leafs to the gazebo a few yards away.

Nieman studied the gazebo's cupola roof. "What's this used for these days?"

"Well, it ain't really used very much at all, but we had an orchestra playing there once. That where Mr. Cole was gonna have Santa visit with local kids," said Pieratt, "but he changed his mind. Some of that wood railing was rottin' away, and he got nervous about getting sued again. We're gettin' sued all the time."

Nieman looked at his watch. "Let's talk more about the gazebo later. We've got to get this whole place painted and fixed up. We've have to give this old lady a makeover, my man. You willing to learn new skills? You help me on this, and I'll look into some training for you, like plumbing and welding, like your former boss promised. Okay?"

"You bet, Mr. Nieman, yes, sir," Pieratt said, shaking his head up and down.

"But right now, I've got an appointment with the mayor. Which way's his office?"

Pieratt pointed down the street, and Nieman left, confident he'd kept a loyal, if not so multiskilled, employee. He'd need all the help he could get, skilled or not, to handle whatever fate awaited the old place, short of the wrecker's ball.

Chapter 10

Cotton Pickin' Lecture

If nothing else, Charles Kash Gomia was a self-made man, and he let everyone know it. Born in Arkansas, he'd say he knew life's hard lessons "from the bottom up." The bottom had been Arkansas's cotton fields. The top, he'd tell visitors, "Well, I guess I haven't reached that yet, but when I die and I'm with the Lord, that's gotta be pretty close to the top, don't you think?"

The oversize owner of the town's largest independent insurance agency liked to be known by his middle name—"but you can spell it with a *C*." He didn't let anyone he met leave without knowing how he managed to work his way up in the world and become the richest man in town at the same time. But he could be counted on for his generosity to charities, as well for public service as mayor and Rotary president.

A black lunch pail stood on the front edge of the polished, plateau-size cherry wood desk at his office. Visitors couldn't help but ask why the richest man in town had a lunch pail on his desk.

"I'm glad you asked," a beaming Gomia would say, leaning far back in his leatherbound executive chair and folding his hands over a fully endowed paunch. He'd say the lunch pail was there so "I won't forget how I got here in the first place." He'd go on to talk about his days as a young man working with his father in the cotton fields of Arkansas, long before the family moved to Indiana. He'd get out of his chair and spread his feet apart on the carpet and lean over to demonstrate how he once picked cotton.

"You'd be grabbin' those cotton bolls from the row to the left with your left hand and then grabbin' more from the row on the right with your other hand. And you'd keep at it, going along between the rows all day long, always bending over, with my daddy right in front of me. Well, at noon we'd get a break and eat a sandwich or two from a lunch pail like that one.

"One day I noticed, way down the field, in the sky there was some dark clouds forming and coming our way. I knew that meant rain and we'd have to stop picking cotton. Well, sir, no young fella really likes to pick cotton, so those clouds were good news, to me and I kept watching them coming closer and closer. When the rain finally fell and we finished up, I weighed my cotton and had only a few pounds instead of what I'd normally pick, a lot more."

"My daddy looked at me and he said, 'Son, I had my eye on you watching those clouds coming, and you slowed down and got slower and slower. That's not how you make money, son,' he'd say. 'You make it by pickin' cotton as fast as you can and forgettin' about what's coming that you can't control. If you just keep on working in life as hard as possible and don't think about nothing else, you'll be making big M-O-N-E-Y,' he'd tell me, spelling out each letter. Before he died my daddy had bought that whole cotton field and had people do the picking for him. 'Gotta' think big, son,' Daddy always told me."

About then, a wise visitor would say he'd just remembered an urgent appointment he had and bid Gomia a goodbye.

The day the new manager of the Silver Swan showed up at Gomia's insurance agency office, the former cotton-picker was on the phone but hung up when his secretary brought Nieman into his office. "Been wanting to meet with you, Mr. Nieman. Have a seat." He gestured toward a large leatherbound couch alongside his expansive desk and shook Nieman's had with a vise grip.

"How'd you like our city now that you've been here a while? Favorably, I hope."

"Oh, yes," said Nieman, slightly uncomfortable in the couch as he sank deeper into its overstuffed leather cushions, finding himself several inches below Gomia's gaze. His own curious gaze was on the shiny black lunch pail.

Gomia folded his arms and sat back in his chair. "I asked you over just so I could meet the new manager of our most famous hotel. As mayor I like to keep up with what's going on in town. The Swan's been an important part of this community forever, but I guess I don't have to tell you that."

"Oh, I've been made aware of the hotel's importance by almost everyone I've met," said Nieman. "I'm happy to be a part of its history. I'm kind of surrounded by it there."

"You sure are. You could open your own antique shop and make more money selling the stuff in your lobby than the hotel makes from overnight guests," said Gomia. "And it's money that makes the world go 'round." He laughed. "Now, you oughta be making friends with our local lady lawyer, named Landrew. She thinks a lot about herself but knows a lot about old furniture and things like that."

Nieman said, "Really? We've met but it wasn't about antiques."

"I bet not," said Gomia with a sly grin. "She's a looker. But, anyway, I need to ask if you'd mind coming to a Rotary luncheon sometime and meet the members."

"Be glad to." A former Rotarian, Nieman was familiar with the club's charitable causes.

"They want to hear about any plans you have for the Swan."

"I can't tell them much, frankly," said Nieman, lying but trying his best to sound sincere. "No plans are set in concrete yet. We're going to fix it up a bit and then see what happens."

"You know, Mr. Nieman," said the mayor, cupping his hands over his stomach and tilting his chair back as far as it would go without falling over, "we're trying hard here to make the town attract more development. We're making our streets better and trying to make our downtown more impressive with what we call economic incentives."

Nieman nodded enthusiastically.

"We think the town's history can put us on the map—make us a destination city again in this part of the state—and the Swan's a big part of the history, so it'd sure be a shame if the rumors of the closing are true."

"Well, as I said, the plans are indefinite right now."

"I understand." Gomia paused. "I should mention something else too. There's a move on to change the name of our city, so we'd get more recognition, be more visible, if you follow me. Plainview is just too … ah, too plain, ha, excuse the pun. Grantville has some zing to it, don't you think? Of course it's meaningful too since the general visited here a number of times."

"I've heard about the name change effort. Local people in favor?"

"Yes, sir," Gomia replied. "Just about everybody's in favor. Because we need some pizzazz around here to attract new business and maybe tourists. That's why losing the Swan would be such a loss."

"Well, I'll pass all that along to my home office. I'm sure they'd be interested in an effort like that in a town with one of their properties."

"Hope you do, sir. Now, can I ask another favor?" said Gomia, taking a drink of water from a glass on his desk. "The Swan's always been one of the sponsors of the homecoming parade the high school puts on. Rotary always helps pay for the floats, and we round up some other sponsors too. It'd be no big cost to you, just a couple hundred bucks. Can we sign you up again? Parade's next week. You don't need a float. We'll take care of you getting attention in the parade."

"Yes, sure. We'd be proud to participate, Mr. Mayor."

"Just call me Kash, son," said the mayor as he rose to shake Nieman's hand. "'Course that's with a *C* you understand." He laughed.

Nieman laughed and turned to leave but hesitated for a moment. He felt compelled to ask about the shiny black lunch pail. When he finally did leave, he was sorry he'd asked.

Chapter 11

Passing Parade

The rat-a-tat and muffled boom-boom of drums coming from a few blocks away held Nieman back from stepping off the curb and crossing the street as police sirens blared. Up early, he'd decided a few days after talking to the mayor to take a walking tour of his new surroundings. Hearing what he guessed was likely the Plainview High School marching band, he was reminded of the school's homecoming game parade and his first attempt at community goodwill for the Swan via Mayor Gomia. He'd ponied up $200 to fulfill his pledge, so he waited to watch the homecoming parade unfold. After all, he'd taken the stroll to catch the flavor of the town.

When members of the football team showed up at his office and he gave them a check, they told him the school art club would make a big Swan banner the freshman cheerleaders would carry in the parade. What he didn't expect, as the band played its fight song and marched by the corner where he stood, were the bold words on the promised banner held high over the heads of four cheerleaders: "Save the Swan." And then they broke into a cheer: "Save the Swan. Save the Swan. *You won't miss it till it's gone.*"

Oh, Jesus, he thought as two of the strutting cheerleaders in front of the banner tossed their spinning batons as they went by. He should have asked for the particulars before the parade. It was too late to complain now. *Thank God no one from the company is here*, he thought. Saving the hotel was the last option for Swinton management.

As the parade passed by, Nieman couldn't help but smile when a short, costumed mascot character accompanying the cheerleaders ambled by in the guise of General Grant. To the delight of the crowd, he waved an oversized replica of a pearl-handled six-shooter in the air. A leather holster was hanging from his hip, and he wore a rumpled blue uniform and a slouchy brimmed hat sporting two big gold stars.

A lady dressed like the Statue of Liberty stood on a platform in a flatbed truck, serving as the Rotary float. Flapping on the side of the trailer a banner read "Grantville for the Future."

Football team members passed by on a decorated float to loud applause, followed by convertibles carrying six homecoming king and queen candidates. He noticed one of the queens rode in a yellow convertible that looked just like the car he'd seen leaving the Swan after Missy Landrew dropped in about that lawsuit. He chuckled, betting himself that most of the money paid for those flashy wheels probably came from her fees for handling suits against the hotel.

As the band music faded and a sheriff's posse on horseback trotted by to end the parade, Nieman headed down another tree-lined street and continued the walking tour of his new venue.

CHAPTER 12

Small-Town Charm

With the strains of the marching band still echoing, Nieman turned down a street lined with well-kept Victorian homes, each with a display of well-maintained gardens on the cusp of losing their season's luster. A lone mother pushed her baby in a stroller with lace-edged canopy along the quiet sidewalk.

The leafy out-reaching canopies of aged red oaks and other tall trees on both sides of the street formed a near perfect branchy arch over the roadway. Picturesque, he thought, but it didn't compare to some near-downtown areas of Atlanta with Civil War hints here and there among tidy antebellum mansions. And were the bougainvillea, rhododendron, and Spanish moss? And the Falcons' new stadium? He'd left Atlanta with unused season tickets, just when the team was having its best year ever.

Crossing the street, Nieman came closer to one stately old home he'd noticed from across the street, and he found himself looking at the town's public library. He glanced at his watch but remembered he was in no hurry. This was Plainview, the slow lane. Forget the downtown Big Peach bustle. Besides, he liked libraries, and not just for reading.

Unlike many of his hospitality colleagues, Nieman had been a regular at Atlanta's downtown public library, finding solace and temporary escape from the frenzied pace of satisfying very picky guests at the elegant Grande Arms.

Like the Swan, the library was an antique, though not as old, he suspected. It was likely once the home of a well-heeled family. He guessed if he stayed around town long enough, he'd eventually hear that family name. He headed to the library.

CHAPTER 13

Dusting Off an Old Book

Nieman stepped into the main room of the library, and before he could look around to get his bearings, a gray-haired lady in a khaki skirt and wearing tiny glasses tiptoed up to him from his side. "Hello. Can we help you find something?" she said, removing the glasses as she spoke.

"Well, hello," said Nieman, taken unawares. "I, uh, I'm new in town and was just taking a look at your library. I do have an interest in history of the area, though."

"Do you mean local history or history of the state of Indiana?" She put two fingers on her chin in a Thinker posture, while cupping her elbow at her waist with the other hand.

"I guess I'm mostly interested in the history of the town. You see, I'm the new manager of the Silver Swan, and the place seems to be so full of the past."

"Well, let me introduce myself," she said, smiling demurely. "I'm Faith Quinton. I used to be the head librarian here. I'm retired now, but I'm here a lot as a volunteer. And your name might be?"

"Lee Nieman," he said, extending his hand and thinking she looked too outdoorsy for a librarian, her face too tan for someone spending her days in the stacks. "I don't want to trouble you, but I was thinking there might be a local history book about the town and maybe something on the hotel too."

She gestured toward the rear of the room, where spiral stairs ascended to the upper floors. A red velvet-encased chain serving as a barrier drooped across the first step of the staircase. On either side of the first step the newel posts were carved with reliefs of maidens in long, flowing gowns twirling in the wind.

"I think you've come to the right place, Mr. Nieman," she said, unlatching one end of the chain and gesturing for him to join her in climbing the steps. "We'll head for the Indiana Room. I spend a lot of time there anyway doing research for my book."

"Oh. You're an author?" he asked as they climbed the steps.

"Well, I hope to be some day," she said. "I'm sorry we're so primitive here."

"Oh, I don't mind. This is a nice old building. Bet it was once a family home?"

"Yes. It's ancient and inefficient, but we love it here."

As they reached the landing, Nieman's imagination took him back to the old days with young debutants in formal ankle-length dresses. He saw them sweeping down this same staircase to greet their escorts for the cotillion, where they'd "come out"in local society and dance with young men of other well-to-do families.

"This could be your lucky day," she said as they walked past several stacks loaded with old hardbacks. "Not only do we have some simply terrific material on local history, but I happen to be the current president of the local historical society."

"Oh, really?"

"Yes, so maybe I can help you there too," she said. "A good deal of local history has revolved around the hotel, as you might have guessed. My father and even my grandfather worked there for many years as managers, so I know some of its secrets too."

Nieman nodded. He'd always been fascinated by local history, although at Atlanta's Emory University he was an English major. The Swan's colorful past seemed some consolation for being stuck here in a job about which he was less than enthusiastic.

"Well, here we are." They stood before a door labeled "Indiana and Plainview History."

The retired head librarian turned toward Nieman, and with a broad smile, she put her glasses back on. "We're very proud of this room. The Norton family once called this mansion their home. Of course that was a long time ago, but the original Norton—Ira Norton—was the founder of the Swan."

"Yes, I remember seeing that name on some documents I looked over before I came to town."

As she reached to an upper shelf for a thick volume with a well-worn cover, Nieman guessed her to be in her seventies but still very perky with a very healthy figure. Her hair was bunched into a not- too-tidy bun in back. As she pulled the book from the shelf, the book adjacent to it came out with it.

"Mercy. Somebody has managed to leave a piece of chewing gum between these two books. Probably some teenager doing a school project. Pity." She pulled the gum off the cover with a tissue and leafed through a few pages of The History of Ross County and Plainview.

"You'll find lots to read in this, and there's a good deal about the hotel in it too. The hotel's the reason our town has had so many famous visitors. But we can also brag about having had a religious sect here and an Indian tribe."

"Indians?"

"Oh, yes. We had the last of a tribe here years ago," she said, handing the book to him. "I remember seeing them out in the country when I was a very little girl, but I suppose they're all gone now."

He headed to a chair by a window, the pane brushed outside by the branches of a towering chestnut tree.

"You probably know that ages ago the hotel was very famous in its day." He detected an eagerness likely stemming from meeting someone other than a school child showing an interest in local history.

"Of course, you've heard of General—or President—Grant being a big name who visited here often, but there were many others who came for lodging, and because the Swan was considered the best dining spot in all of Indiana. Quite a few people traveled here on the way to Louisville and Chicago and, of course, Indianapolis.

"And then there was the Underground Railroad too, Mr. Nieman. Plainview played a major role in that before the Civil War. You can find homes all over town that still have underground hideaways they used to keep whole slave families out of sight overnight and sometimes for days."

"I've heard about that," said Nieman as he settled into the big leather-covered chair and opened the book she'd given him

"Thanks so much, Miss Quinton."

"Remember now, if I can be of any help, just call me here. They know where to find me, which is usually here or at home with my birds. Bye."

Birds? He wondered what she meant but blew off a coating of dust from the top of the old tome and began thumbing through the many dog-eared pages.

Chapter 14

A Must for Travelers

Nieman had scanned several chapters in the book and was about to leave the library when a passage caught his eye.

Nearby, a community of Shakers blossomed in the mid-1800s, but the community and the sect began shrinking in numbers. By the middle of the twentieth century, the group near here had all but vanished, as had the other centers of the faith in Ohio and Pennsylvania.

Plainview can also boast in its past an Indian tribe, the Chikopiks, who lived by the local river of the same name. Years ago, but even up until the 1950s, these Indians could sometimes be found walking city streets and dealing with local merchants. But like the Shakers, the tribe dwindled, and by the mid-twentieth century, almost no tribe members were known to be living in the Plainview area.

He scanned a few more chapters and stumbled on one about the hotel itself.

> Built in 1838 by Ira Norton, who had come to town as an immigrant from Scotland, the Swan opened its doors in 1839 and was an instant success with the traveling public. It flourished well into the mid-1900s as a very prestigious and even luxurious rest stopover for travelers with money who had come by coach from Chicago and Indianapolis and other cities in Ohio, Kentucky, and Indiana.
>
> The best wines were served, and the chef for many of those early years apparently was hired by Norton away from a top Chicago dinner club. During the final decades of the 1800s and into the early 1900s, the Swan was put on the map as a "must" stop for travelers who could afford it. Critics came from Chicago and even St. Louis and found much to rave about in Swan dinner menus.

Reading on, he found many of the names who'd been overnight hotel guests: P. T. Barnum, Wild Bill Hickok, Charles Dickens, Indiana's famed poet James Whitcomb Riley, and Ulysses S. Grant. The general, according to the author, "was not an infrequent guest, along with his staff during lulls in the Civil War. The Swan's owner was always happy to supply the general and his companions with their needs in whiskey, wine, and food as they relaxed, often playing cards far into the night."

This is the good stuff of history, Nieman thought as he scanned more pages and found himself reading about the Swan's connections with the pre–Civil War Underground Railroad that assisted fugitive slaves. His eyes were riveted on one passage: "And the Swan proudly did its part too in those years under the Norton family ownership. It is believed that several passages built with the owner's encouragement still exist beneath the hotel, but they were all sealed for safety's sake."

One chapter was devoted to the alleged Swan ghost, attributing her appearance to "the imaginations of city dwellers sleeping in the quiet atmosphere of the Swan in a small town so far from the harsh din of big city life."

Nieman rose from the chair to leave but couldn't get the "underground passages" out of his mind. He quickly descended the stairs and spotted Faith Quinton, who was chatting with a departing patron.

"Miss Quinton, thank you so much for showing me around, but I do have a question. The book mentions underground passages. Have you ever heard of there being any at the hotel?"

"It's been rumored for years around town that there were, indeed, some underground passages there, but I think most were filled in long ago," she said.

Nieman thanked her and left, wondering if an expedition to the Swan's cellar would satisfy his curiosity. Or was it even worth the effort? After all, he wasn't planning on a lifelong career here. But he was beginning to admit to a growing fascination with the state's oldest hotel—and likely its most dilapidated.

Chapter 15

Can't Refuse an Offer

The next morning Nieman decided to put off any sortie to the Swan's cellar and head to the county recorder's office. His boss back in Atlanta had told him to fix the problem with the Swan's deed, if he could.

But he had an errand to run before heading to the county seat.

As he parallel parked at the curb outside Missy Landrew's law office, behind her shiny, canary yellow, late-model Mustang convertible, he felt a momentary twinge of embarrassment. His '78 Mercedes not only showed all of its 185,000 miles, but its noisy diesel engine and the noxious exhaust odor were hard to hide.

Before he could open his car door, Plainview's female attorney, dressed in a tight three-piece business suit, popped out of her office door and headed for her convertible.

"Hi there," a surprised Nieman, half out of his car, shouted at her, waving a handful of documents he'd brought with him.

"Well, hello. What are you doing in this end of town? Slumming?"

"No. I thought this was the nicer end of town. After all, where I work everything is a century and a half old."

"Like that antique you're driving?" She pursed her lips, feigning a smirk. "Just kidding. I kind of wish I still had my old Honda instead of this thing. It's my brother's, but he went in the army and let me use it till he gets back. He likes muscle cars."

"Three-eight vee six?"

"Why, Mr. Nieman, I wouldn't have guessed. You know cars? You don't seem the type."

"I'm not. I just know a little about Mustangs because I had one once. But my father was big on older cars. He left me this one when he died last year."

She opened the passenger side door of her car and threw her briefcase on the seat. "This one has a vee-eight under the hood. We're talking zero to sixty in under six seconds with this baby. That's how they advertised it."

"I just can't get over a lady lawyer in a yellow GT convertible—with a spoiler yet. You must have really made an impression on the legal community around here when you started driving that around. Why not just add racing stripes?" he said.

"Like I told you: anything to impress the local legal eagles. You here just to discuss my wheels?"

"Actually, no," he said, handing her the sheath of papers. "It was just coming over to see you. I'm sure you're in a hurry, so I'll just drop these off with your secretary. They're about that lady and the tripping thing. I've got all the agreements signed by the big shots in Atlanta. I'm headed to the county seat."

"What a coincidence. I'm going to the county seat too. Got to talk turkey with a judge. How long are you going to be there?"

Caught off guard, Nieman said, "Ah, well, I need to look at some old deeds in the recorder's office. Probably take an hour. Why?"

"I was just thinking I could show you a little southern Indiana hospitality and offer you a ride there. I won't be there long."

"Oh, ah, I don't know," muttered Nieman. "I really should finish a job I just started back at the hotel."

"Bet you could do it later. Besides," she said, as she tied her hair back and hopped into her car, "I'll drive you there, but you can buy lunch for us. You know, it isn't every day I go around picking up men off the street and offering them a ride."

"I'll take your word for that," he said, thinking the last thing he needed right now was a woman in his life, but he hopped into her car, and she hit the ignition switch.

The Mustang lurched away from the curb. Nieman's head was jerked back against the headrest. Landrew turned toward him with a grin and said, "Well, it's supposed to be a fun car too, isn't it? "

Nieman, a speed-limit driver, put a tight grip on his knees as she ignored the signs for twenty-five miles per hour along Main Street, turning the heads of some pedestrians ambling along the sidewalks and keeping him pressed back into the leather seat at every shift of the stick transmission. He hoped she wouldn't demonstrate the "sixty in six" until they were out of town.

CHAPTER 16

Speaking of Antiques

The speedometer needle of her Mustang hovered at seventy-five as Missy Landrew negotiated the curves and dipping hills of the back road leading to the county seat. She slipped a Karen Carpenter tape into the player and leaned back in the seat. "How do you like our little patch of southern Indiana by now?" she asked.

Nieman was lost in thought as the fall colors of the woods on both sides of the highway blurred in passing. "This is beautiful country around here. It reminds me of my home area in Pennsylvania. I guess I still miss Atlanta, though, and the Smokies. Ever been there?"

"No. Our family has always gone to Colorado for vacations," she replied, her tied-back auburn hair blowing back in the wind stream. Neither spoke for a few miles as they listened to her tape of pop tunes.

As "Close to You" ended she turned to him and said, "Speaking of Atlanta, how is it you ended up here? You didn't choose to come here, did you? I wouldn't think this would be the glamor end of the hotel business. I heard that you ran a very big hotel there."

"Yes, I guess I did," he replied, feeling a touch of nostalgic bitterness. "It's a long story."

"We've got a half hour before we get there."

He told her of his involvement with Atlanta's urban renewal program and how he had joined a citizen group that pushed for saving a classic 1920s downtown building adjacent to the lavish Grande Arms he managed. He hadn't known at the time that Swinton had the same property in mind for an expansion of the Grande Arms for high- priced suites, tennis courts, and a club room. But the citizen group prevailed, and Swinton was shut out.

"So I wind up running the Swan, a property the company isn't very interested in, to be frank." He turned back to gazing at the passing countryside, mostly miles of soft, rolling forested hills and recently shorn corn and bean fields.

"So, you have a thing for saving heritages?"

"Kind of. I like history."

"You're in a good spot for that. Not many hotels have a history like the Swan's. Just the antiques alone are like a storehouse of history. I don't suppose you're into antiques, though, are you?"

"Not really, but it sounds like you are."

"Oh, yes, antiques are one of my fun pastimes. But I'm no expert. I've only bought a few, but I have relatives in the business."

"You know," he said, "I wonder if you wouldn't mind coming over to the hotel some day and telling me about some of the furniture and things we have there, like in the lobby. I'd like to straighten up the clutter and be able to tell people staying there what the old things are all about, maybe redecorate a little at the same time."

"Sure, I'd love to. That'd be fun. For example, I bet you don't know about that long, skinny table by the fire place that you see every time you walk through the lobby."

"Don't know. I've wondered."

"It's an undertaker's table a local funeral home used to work on dead bodies." She laughed as she negotiated a sharp turn.

"No kidding?" said Nieman as they passed the city limits sign of the county seat. She slowed to fifty, and he relaxed.

"You've got a treasure trove of value just in the lobby alone. And there's some real art on the walls … and that butter churn in the lobby and that Kentucky long rifle mounted over the fireplace. I've always wondered why no one has ever swiped one or the other, or a piece of antique furniture or art or something."

"Hadn't thought about that."

"Yeah. Take the Shaker chairs in some of the rooms, for example. They're authentic and worth a bundle of money. And who knows what's in the rest of the place. You been in the old ballroom yet?"

"No, but I've been told by Handley there's a real jumble of old stuff that's just been stored there for years."

"The story," she said as they approached the courthouse, "is that the owners over the years always bought the best furniture and all the stuff that comes with running a top-rated hotel. They hardly even threw anything out. But styles change, so a lot of things were stored upstairs and never came out again."

"It might be interesting to do some exploring up there."

"It'd be more than interesting," she said as she pulled into the courthouse parking lot. "Just call me when you're ready to go up and look around—no consulting fee, I promise."

"Hey," he said, getting out of the car, "that'd have to be a first for an attorney."

"Bad joke, Mr. Nieman," she said as they began the climb up the steps to the entrance. She shook her head back and forth and ran her fingers through her hair to untangle it from the windblown ride.

Nieman noticed the late morning sunlight brought out a hint of red in her copper-hued hair.

"Meet back here in an hour? We can grab a sandwich and head home, okay?"

"Right," he said as he pulled open the big courthouse door for her and headed to the recorder's office.

Chapter 17

What Indians?

Their slider and fries lunch didn't take much time. Landrew had a client scheduled at 2:30, and Nieman was anxious to check out something he'd spotted in the Swan's property deed at the recorder's office. The ride back to Plainview was uneventful. They chatted about their respective families. She talked about her more interesting legal cases, and he talked about his teen twin daughters he hoped to see soon on a visit back to Atlanta.

Missy pulled her convertible in front his Mercedes by her office.

"Thanks again for the trip," he said, opening the car door while clutching his briefcase with the deed papers he'd brought from the recorder's office. "Maybe lunch again sometime?"

"Yeah, maybe." As he stepped to the curb, she added, "Want to run some morning? I run with a group at the city park."

"Ah, well, I guess. Sure. I have been getting out of shape since coming here."

"We do a mile or so Saturday at the state park. Too much for you?"

"Very funny. I'm not that out of shape. Unlike lawyering, I don't just sit around and shuffle papers."

"Touché, Mr. Nieman. And thank you for lunch, and the signed papers too. I'm sure my client will be so happy."

"She ought to be," he said. "Twenty thousand for falling on the floor—Mrs. Coolridge should be happy as hell."

"And don't forget to call me when you want to show me all the old stuff at the hotel—and maybe the ghost."

They both laughed.

"I'm not sure I can dredge her up, but I'll give you all the antiques you'll ever want to see." He waved and hurried to drive back to the Swan.

Nieman gazed across the hotel's wide yard for a few minutes and decided to take a few casual measurements. He began walking to the rear of the property, taking long strides. He knew his strides were about three feet and counted them as he moved across the lawn, passing the gazebo and wishing pond. He looked for a benchmark in the ground but didn't see one. He pulled a pen from his pocket and began scribbling some numbers in a notepad. Something was wrong. He paced off the distance again in the opposite direction. He jotted down more figures, studied the tract map the recorder had given him, and stood puzzled.

"Something's off," he said out loud, staring at the hotel grounds. Something just didn't add up. He'd paced off 160 feet, but the lot was described as being only 150 feet from east to west. He took a closer look at the map and noticed two faint parallel lines forming about a ten-foot-wide strip bisecting the tract, running across the Swan's property near the gazebo and pond. The diagram's handwritten notation on the narrow strip was too small to read, though he could read the "Swinton" designation on the two main sections of the grounds on either side of the strip. He pulled his car key ring out of his pocket. Besides his apartment and car keys, it held a tiny magnifying glass.

Now he could read the notation. "Tribal designation. Chikopik Nation, registered US Bureau of Indian Affairs." He read it again. An Indian tribe? Were these the same Indians Faith Quinton was talking about? Was this the "glitch" that held up issuance of a clean land title all this time? Where are all these Indians now?

"Hello, Faith?" Nieman asked after rushing to his office and phoning the library. She was off so he was given her home phone number.

"This is Lee Nieman at the hotel. Remember, we met a couple of weeks ago and you showed me the history books on Plainview?"

"Of course, I remember you, Mr. Nieman. How can I help you?"

"You mentioned when I was there something about Indians living around this area a long time ago. Could you tell me again the name of the tribe?"

"Oh, yes, of course. Around here probably everybody my age or older remembers the Indians being here. I think they've all disappeared now—died off, you know—but they were called the Chikopiks, and they lived on the other side of the creek that I live on. It's named after those Indians: Chikopik Creek. Runs into the Ohio."

"I'll be," said Nieman. "Thanks so much."

"You mind my asking why you're so interested?"

"Well, I have a map of the Swan's property. and it shows that the tribe still has a claim on a little strip of land there. Kind of curious, isn't it?"

"It certainly is. Oh, when I was a very little girl I remember seeing what my father told me were Indians down by the river where I live now, and I've read that they were close with the Shaker colony here. I certainly didn't know they still owned land at the hotel, or anywhere around town. Can't imagine. I'll have to do a little research on that."

"Okay. I'd like to know more too. It's got my curiosity up."

"You might want to come down to my house some day and see where I think that tribe used to live."

"Yes, I might take you up on that offer this weekend. I'll give you a call, and thanks again, Faith. As usual you've been very helpful."

"Anytime, Mr. Nieman. Bye now."

Chapter 18

Rock-Solid Home

With some effort, Faith Quinton pushed her aging body up from the low rock wall she was sitting on, cupped her hand to her mouth, and shouted down toward the creek by her house.

"Bobby boy! You can bring up a few more now, and then you can go on home if you like. There's always tomorrow."

The object of her shouting, Bobby Kemper, a freshman and football player at Plainview High School, looked up from where he was kneeling over the water's edge, trying to pry a large rock up from the creek bed.

"Yes, ma'am, I'm just trying to get one more before I quit." He knew the more rocks he lugged up the bank to her house, the more money he'd make.

In her at-home khaki slacks, white sneakers, and sun visor, with her binoculars hanging from her neck on a lanyard, Faith looked more the bird watcher she was than a librarian. She was, in fact, both, which added to her being a Plainview legend in her own time. People in town knew her well, not only as the local bird aficionado and retired head librarian but because of the rock house she called home—and how it was built.

Everyone knew the widow Quinton had built her house with rocks carried up the steep bank of the creek by her several late husbands. Since her last husband died, she'd been forced to pay high schoolers to do the work because she needed more rocks for a planned addition.

Her legend, however, reached even further into the roots of the town. Her grandfather and then her father had both worked in management at the Swan. Her father once thought about buying it but quit when the remaining heir to the property, Sylvia Norton, began interfering in operations.

"Bobby, that'll do for the day, but I'd like to see you back here tomorrow," Faith said as the sturdy youth climbed up the bank, lugging two Frisbee-sized stones. "Always remember, Bobby, that more important than the money you're earning, is that you're learning how man works with nature for mutual benefits."

"Yes, ma'am, a better purpose." He'd heard it all before. "Thanks, but now I have to go to football practice." He waved, jogged up the hill behind the rock house, and vanished into a thick clutch of maples and poplars that shielded the house from the busy highway to Plainview.

In her house Faith found her dog lying in his favorite place on the couch. "Well, Mr. Duke, we have to get busy: comb our hair, straighten up the place, and talk about the old days with the new boss at the Silver Swan." She moved toward the bathroom, still talking to the dog, now with only one eye still open. "I just wish they'd get it back to what it used to be. Oh, those were the days, Mr. Duke. You would've loved it."

She looked in her bathroom mirror, unwrapped the bandana to let a bundle of alabaster hair tumble around her shoulders, and began brushing it.

"Just the same, I wish he were an older gentleman," she told the dog, now asleep with both eyes closed. "We surely do need help around here—on a longer-term basis—since that pitiful excuse for a husband died ... dumb drunk."

CHAPTER 19

Fond Memories

Nieman craned his neck to look up at the purple martin nesting houses at the top of metal poles. He'd seen these multi-bird dwellings with quarter-size access holes at homes in Atlanta and always wondered why anyone would go to all that trouble just for birds.

No one answered his knock on Faith Quinton's door, and he didn't see anyone around the house on the high creek bank. He stood there, gazing at the place with hummingbird feeders hanging from the porch eve, concluding that the rock house looked more like a Revolutionary War fortress than a home.

"Hello, hello, Mr. Nieman. I'm coming. I'm coming." Her voice came from the trees in back of her house. He couldn't see her at first, but when she finally approached, binoculars bouncing around her neck, he noticed her white hair was no longer in the bun he'd seen at the library. It was down and tied to one side with a yellow ribbon and a flower.

"I'm so sorry I wasn't here when you came—checking my feeders out back. You know, cold weather isn't far off. I want the poor dears to know they can always get something to eat here."

Nieman smiled, not sure he wanted to get too far into a conversation about birds.

Abruptly, she cocked her head toward some scrub brush near the house as she approached him. "Hear that? Oh, isn't that sweet."

"Pardon?"

"That was my little wren singing."

"Hmm," Nieman said, trying to sound interested.

Her gaze turned to the creek bank and beyond. He noticed the slogan embossed on the back of her windbreaker: "Condors Forever."

"Now, you know those Indians I told you about, the Chikopiks? I think about them sometimes when winter's coming. Can you imagine how cold they must have been, just living in tents and lean-tos. They're all gone now, I guess, but my grandfather used to tell me about them. I remember once he said they didn't talk to him a lot."

She pointed across the creek to a broad fallow field edged by a copse of trees a half-mile or so distant and raised her binoculars. "That's where they lived. Once in a while, when I was a little girl, I'd come down here with a friend to explore. We'd see some of the young Indians fishing in the creek. We were told they called themselves the 'warriors.' We'd wave at them, and they'd wave back. No one there now, though."

"I imagine."

"Oh, by the way, I did a little more research and found out that a very long time ago the tribe did have an encampment for years where the Swan is today."

"Oh really?"

"Yes, the village ceded the tribe a small piece of property there as a consolation for being pushed out here in the country."

"Well, I'll be damned. That's what I saw in the deed."

"Kind of sad, isn't it? Kick them out and leave them a little piece of ground that was worthless to them."

"It is, but at least you wound up with nice memories out here. I imagine that plus all this natural beauty is why you chose to live here?"

"Yes, yes, it was. It's so beautiful, especially in the fall."

They turned toward her home. "This is an amazing house you have here. Must have taken years to build," Nieman said.

He'd been told the house took very hard labor by her several husbands lugging the flat rocks up the bank. It got a bit larger with each husband, depending on his enthusiasm for the job, or lack of.

"Well, it has taken a long time, but I'm not through yet," she said, gesturing toward the Adirondack chairs on the wide veranda. "Why don't we just sit out here and talk? Would you like a soda or coffee?"

He declined the offer and said, "It's been a long time since I've sat in one of these."

"Oh, they're wonderful, except the older you get the harder it is to get back up and out of them," she said. "You know, these came from the Swan's lawn. They were shipped here from the east. The Norton family liked things to be authentic—they even used real Wedgwood china for years for special guests. Don't know what happened to it all, but it's probably all stored there somewhere.

"They liked to save everything too. That's why there are so many antiques at the hotel. Heck, some of my furniture came from the Swan before they sold it to your company. My daddy was given some pieces when he managed the place."

She went on. "The house started with my first husband, Geoffrey, God love him. He just carried rock after rock up here for years, and then he got back trouble. He was a good man. They were all good men—with one exception, the last one.

"All four of them died with complications from back problems, hernias, ruptures, herniated disks, that sort of thing. Poor souls"

"Can't imagine why," Nieman said with a wry smile.

"Oh, I think all the hard work kept them in shape—except the last one drank too much and didn't do a lick of work on the house. But he lived longer than all the others."

"A lesson in life, you think?" He tried not to sound too sarcastic.

"Well maybe, but I'm sure you didn't come out here to listen to the painful story of my marital history."

"No, but I have to admit yours is the best one I've heard recently."

Chapter 20

Those Were the Days

Faith didn't mind talking about the years her grandfather, and then her father, were managers at the Swan. For a long time as a youngster she was "the darling" of the hotel staff, as she put it.

"Oh, it was a wonderful place to be back then. My father started out as head of food service. When they had cakes and pies left over, he'd bring some home for us.

"Daddy was general manager for a few years but he and Miss Norton—she's the great-granddaughter of the founder, you know—got into arguments about how to operate the hotel. So he went into teaching."

"I bet you had some good memories of those years."

"Oh, yes. When I was very little and my grandfather was in charge, I remember being around when all the staff was getting ready for big fancy parties that were held in the ballroom on the fourth floor, after dinner downstairs. There were concerts, and often debutants would have their cotillions there. Sometimes I'd sit on the ballroom floor at the bottom of the long, dark blue velvet drapes with gilded fringes and watch the people coming and going.

"Once a British duke and duchess came for dinner. He wore a bright red uniform, and I remember thinking how dashing he looked. I expected him to leap on a white horse and wave a sabre in the air."

"Quite a sight, eh?" Nieman said.

"You know, in those days the Swan's chefs had been trained in cities like Chicago, and people would come from all over just for dinner. Of course, that was a long time ago." She dabbed her eye with a tissue.

"Did you ever meet some of the famous people who were hotel guests?"

"Oh, yes, but mostly I just watched. I met Ernest Hemingway, and our state's very famous poet James Whitcomb Riley read "Little Orphant Annie" to me in the lobby. Now when I was a teenager, Mr. P. T. Barnum stayed here overnight once when he was taking his circus to Louisville." Faith continued to tear up as she spoke.

"Well, those really were the days, weren't they? What a wonderful childhood you had."

"Yes, I suppose I did, but that was when the hotel was in its heyday. It really hasn't been the same since then, and things have gotten worse—excuse me for saying it—since your big company took over. But that's the way of big business, I guess. Tradition doesn't matter. I just hope the day will come when someone will take that place and restore it to what it used to be, when it was the grandest hotel in southern Indiana, in the Midwest maybe. That'd be something my family and everybody in town would be proud of—even if they do change the town name to Grantville."

"Do you think people in town would like to have the Swan restored to its old glory?"

"Oh, yes. You know, for some of us, old has its own charms. I think everyone in town would like to see it restored, except maybe someone like Sylvia Norton. She's the main heir of the Norton family founder, you know."

"That's what I understand." He remembered his boss telling him something else about Sylvia Norton, but he couldn't recall what it was.

"I hear she's very much against restoring it in any fashion."

"Really?" Nieman asked.

"Oh, she's a hard-nosed one to be sure and says the Swan is now so rundown that it's a blot on her family name. She wants it gone."

"She must be a real proud woman."

"I'd use another word for what she is, Mr. Nieman, but if you ever talk to her, you'll find out what I mean."

"Hard to deal with, eh?"

"Well, let me put it this way. Rather than spending time with Sylvia, most folks around here would probably prefer an ice water enema."

They shared a laugh over that and then Faith leaned toward him and knitted her eyebrows. "But from what I hear, your company is going to tear it down. Is that right? That would be very sad."

He knew she'd ask the question, and he had his "corporate answer" ready. "I really don't know at this point. We are trying to sell it—so far without success."

"Well, I just hope whoever buys it takes care of it because of what it has meant to the town. Our newspaper said when your company bought it that the Norton family—Sylvia—somehow retained a small interest in it."

"Didn't know that. Guess I should have a talk with her sometime."

"Well, you'll find her very difficult to talk to, that snobby woman. Thinks she's still the belle of the ball around here. Snubs everybody in town. Even me."

"Hmm. Well, I'll try. But first I have to find out about the tribe mentioned on the deed."

"Well, I don't know how you're going to deal with dead Indians."

"I've written to the Bureau of Indian affairs to see how to deal with it. The company has asked me to get it cleared up."

"My grandfather said a very long time ago the hotel had some dealings with the tribe, but I'm not sure what it was all about. But certainly they've all died out by now."

"You may be right," he said.

"I certainly hope you can work it out. The Swan was such a personal part of my family's history. I guess it brings out my sentimental side."

"I'm sure it does, but I did want to ask you about whether your grandfather ever said anything about General Grant staying at the Swan? Or was that before his time?"

"Well," Faith said, "I know the family history pretty well, and apparently the general came a number of times during the Civil War. My grandmother told me the general actually came through here and stayed at the Swan before the war. I've researched this for my book, and I've found that Grant never came back here after the war, when he was president. You sure you don't want an iced tea or something?"

"No, thanks. I'm just enjoying the history lesson."

"Well," she continued, "they said that Grant was just a young officer when he stayed there the first time. He was heading out West. But during the war he came with other officers, and usually they'd get into a big poker game up in the ballroom."

Nieman chuckled and said, "But I've heard he drank too much maybe."

"Well, could be. I think that's been exaggerated. My grandfather was told the Swan always stocked the general's favorite wines and especially French brandy. And Grant always ordered the best food on the menu back then, when they had a big name chef working in the kitchen.

"As I understand it, during the war he came whenever things got boring in the war, particularly at Vicksburg, which I guess took the union forever to capture."

"It was a long siege," Nieman said, recalling his American history class.

"My grandfather told my father that the general was a very nice man, very gentlemanly, was always very respectful of the hotel staff. He paid his bill when he came and never drank to excess."

"Wow, that's really interesting. Those would have been fascinating days to work at the hotel," said Nieman, glancing at his watch and rising from the porch chair. "I'd like to hear more, but I'm afraid I'm running out of time."

"Before you leave, can I ask how Mr. Pieratt is these days? He's such a dear man. He came out here one day last summer and pitched in to help carry rocks for my addition. He is divorced now, isn't he?"

"Boney?" Nieman said awkwardly, eyebrows raised. "He's fine. Ah, I don't know if he's divorced. But he's a very helpful guy for us to have around. I've certainly enjoyed talking to you. Can we get together again sometime?"

"Oh, yes, but aren't you going to ask me about the ghost?" said Faith as she rose from the divan. "Everyone else always does."

"I forgot about it. Is there really one there?"

"Oh, yes, I certainly believe so, but that's something I never tell anyone about. It's a secret that I'm holding for my book. And nowadays I'm one of the few people in town who know who the ghost really was—or is—and what she's all about."

"That's some secret. I'll look forward to reading your book."

"Oh, I hope you will," she said as she stepped off the porch with him.

As he opened his car door, she said, "Since you've been so nice, I will let you in on one thing about the ghost: It's all kind of a *family* secret, but the family in question isn't mine. Bye now."

Nieman drove off. *What a sly old gal,* he thought. *No wonder she could snare four husbands, all with muscles and willing to work.*

Chapter 21

A Profitless Deal

Nieman drove directly back to his carriage house apartment, avoiding the hotel all together. It had been a long day with Faith Quinton, and he was nagged by the mention of Sylvia Norton's name. It wasn't too late to call his boss in Atlanta.

"Bob? This is Lee. Are you busy? This'll just take a few minutes."

"No, I'm good. What's up? You going to tell me you finally made a profit on that place?"

"Not exactly. No. I just want you to tell me again about that woman out here, Sylvia Norton. I know you told me her family held some stock in Swinton, but there was something else you said."

"Well, I've never met her, but everybody says she's kind of a crotchety old babe and she writes letters to our CEO from time to time, pleading with him to tear down the hotel."

"Yeah, that's what I'm hearing out here, and I've thought about calling her just for the sake of goodwill."

"Sure. Good idea. Now, her family did get a few hundred Swinton shares when we bought the place, but they got something else as a kind of incentive to sell: 10 percent of the Swan's net profit annually."

"Really?"

"Yeah, but she hasn't gotten a check in years. After all, 10 percent of zero is still zero. As you know, there's practically been no profit since we bought the place. But there's more."

"It gets worse?"

"Kind of. She thinks that 10 percent would apply to any new owner. We don't think so, but she's said she'd take it to court."

"Why would she want it torn down?"

"Well, she'd get a no-hassle return. If the place is torn down and the lot's sold, she'd get 10 percent of the proceeds. And at the same time, she gets rid of the object of her family's so-called embarrassment. And she's also against restoring it because, in her mind, then it would end up just being cheap imitation of its former glorious self, so to speak."

"All that's going to be a nasty fly in the ointment to anybody trying to buy it."

"For sure. But why'd you ask?"

"I'm not sure. I guess it's because the longer I'm here the more interesting the place gets. You know, all its history, and it does have a certain charm." He was beginning to think beyond that now but held back.

"Well, don't get too attached. We have had a couple of nibbles."

"Oh? What's the company asking for it?" "About $425,000. You want to make an offer?" Prestik said.

"It's a possibility ... maybe."

They talked for a few more minutes before signing off.

CHAPTER 22

Last Indian Standing

In the morning at his office, Nieman was greeted as usual with a stack of mail, which he normally would look at later in the day. But he couldn't ignore one return address: US Bureau of Indian Affairs.

Manager, Silver Swan Inn
Plainview, Indiana

Dear Mr. Nieman:

We have researched the question you asked of Native American tribes in the Southern Indiana region of present-day Plainview in the 1700s and 1800s. Our research department has concluded that the Chikopik tribe was the dominant tribe in that area but in modest numbers during most of those decades before and for several decades after the arrival of the first white settlers and traders. However, there existed some Native Americans with other tribal affiliations in scattered locations in the general area, such as the Potawatomi, Delaware, and possibly Miami tribes.

As to whether or not any members of the Chikopik tribal family are still living, we can only say that our records indicate the last living Chikopik likely died in recent years. And we have had no contact with any other member of the tribe, suggesting that no Chikopiks are still alive today.

Our records show that the last member of the tribal family was known as "Indian Joe" or "He of the Long Feather" or Tom Eagleman. He was said to be of very advanced age when the last contact was made with our agency. That was in 1996. His reported age at that time was eighty-seven, and he was a resident of the city of Indianapolis. He had been receiving some government assistance at the time, but that was discontinued when our disbursement division in 1996 began receiving returned mailings. Little else about him is known to our agency, except that, like most young members of the tribe, he was educated in the Shaker colony, which at the time existed near your community.

So as you might imagine, by now he would likely be deceased, but that's only a studied assumption by our researchers.

If we can be of any further assistance, please let us know. Our agency's sole purpose is to assure the continued welfare of all of our Native American population.

Cordially,
Richard Montcalm
Manager, Research
Bureau of Indian Affairs
Washington, DC

CHAPTER 23

Soiling the Family Image

Nieman drummed his fingers on his desk as he sat and waited for Sylvia Norton to show up. The clock showed 10:20 a.m., and Sylvia Norton had said she'd be there at 10:00 a.m.

He had planned to contact her, but she'd called him first and asked to see him, without explaining why. He suspected conversation would likely speak to her desire to see the hotel torn down. Nieman had been forced to cool his heels for perceived dignitaries many times over the years and learned long ago that VIPs liked to make callers wait. It had something to do with control. Nieman knew in this town she was a VIP, one who held a key to any sale of the Swan.

Nieman also knew he'd eventually have to talk Norton into parting with the family's 10 percent deal. No prospective buyer would accept a profit bite like that on a new venture.

He just wished she'd show so he could at least get one problem over with. She might be only one of two obstacles in the path of a sale. He hadn't told his boss yet about the Indian tribe mentioned in the land deed and the possibility that one tribe member might still be alive and kicking somewhere.

Nieman balled up a scrap of paper from his desk, pitched it into the wastebasket across the room, and wondered about the missing Indian, if he existed. Finally, he heard the front door open.

Tall and ever erect, Sylvia Norton walked through the front door of the Swan. In her some eighty years she'd seldom worn slacks and when she did they were never tight-fitting. On this cool autumn day she had donned her usual ankle-length black chiffon dress with a pearl necklace.. It was said around town that when she attended the parochial high school near Plainview, she preferred a knee-length tennis skirt to shorts in physical education classes. Even during her four years at an exclusive college in Pennsylvania, the coed from Indiana could usually be found in a skirt and blouse — never, "God forbid," as she put it then — in the leg-revealing Bermudas worn by a few daring coeds. New fashions eluded her.

She had only dated briefly, remarking to her college dormitory roommates that she found men too "animal-like." She said she was "tired of the men just pawing over me all the time."

As the spinster doyen of the Nortons, she let no one forget that the hotel her great-grandfather had founded was not the same entity that stood there now but only a tattered relic that "no longer reflects the proud heritage" of her ancestry. Her fidelity to the family lineage was such that when she reached adulthood, she had her own surname legally changed to that of her great-grandfather.

When Norton approached the front desk, the clerk was taken aback for a moment. He recognized her but hadn't expected to find himself face to face with the town's best-known and presumably richest senior citizen. "Ah ... I'll get him right away," he stammered as he called Nieman on the intercom.

CHAPTER 24

A Matter of Status

Sylvia, gloved hands folded, stood in her seamed nylons and waited, black-fox fur lining her coat collar, her black skirt nearly reaching her high-top Dr. Scholl orthotics, and her silvered hair perfectly coiffed in a puffy bouffant do from the sixties, with not an idle strand hanging loose. Always impatient, she gazed at the grandfather clock on the wall and tried not to appear too interested in the mixed-period jumble of furnishings crowding the lobby that once buzzed with local dignitaries and visiting travelers of means.

She remembered running through the lobby as a young girl in a frilly dress, rushing through a crowd of well-dressed people to see her grandfather, who always gave her candy from a big glass jar when she visited him at work. He'd always tell her, "Sylvia, my dear girl, you are just so beautiful. Always remember, you are a Norton, and you'll always have something to look up to in your heritage and family lineage."

"Miss Norton, I assume," Nieman said as he came out of his office, extending his hand and guiding her toward his office. "I'm Lee Nieman. Sorry to keep you waiting. So happy to finally meet you. Please have a seat."

Before she sat, Norton looked over at the well-worn chair with the scooped back and fabric seat. "That was one of my father's favorite chairs when he managed the hotel, you know."

"Well, I didn't know that, but if you'd like to take it home, I think we could arrange that."

"No, thank you, Mr. Newman," she said dismissively as they sat.

"Ah, no, it's Nieman," he said, tapping his knee. "As in knee-man."

"No matter, young man. I already have two of these chairs in my home they're Klismos-Form chairs made in Philadelphia. Prized by collectors—but you wouldn't appreciate that, of course."

"I readily admit my ignorance of antiques."

"Of course you do, poor boy," she said. "The antiques world is reserved for those who marvel at the caring workmanship and discerning tastes of the past. My ancestors spared no expense in hotel furnishings. Only the best would do. The only way to live, of course."

"Of course, ah ... for those with an adequate checkbook," he said, trying to lighten the conversation.

"Oh piffle. In any case, in recent years that dedication to high quality and correctness has been, shall we say, compromised. No one with your hotel chain has ever understood anything about this hotel's legacy. Oh, this place has become a positive eyesore—which is what brings me to you."

She stopped in midsentence and looked at him intently for a moment. "Would you be a Princeton man by chance? Certainly Ivy League. I have so many friends who are, you see."

"No, I graduated from Emory Univers—"

"Emory? Oh. Is that one of those correspondence schools?

"No, it's a—"

"Never mind. I attended Bryn Mawr, and I still keep in contact with my classmates in New York and Philadelphia.

Many are married into the leading families of those cities, you know. Well, in any case, let me be direct with you."

"By all means. I think you should if—"

"What you think is immaterial to me, young man. It's what you're going to do here that concerns me. I am, as you may know, the direct heir of the original founder of the Swan. And, of course, I still have a material interest in the business."

"Ahem, yes. I'm familiar with the hotel's history and your, ah, interest."

"Good. Now you will find I'm very well informed, and many of my close friends in the Indianapolis social register tell me you may be here to take down the Swan. Well, I want you and your company's board to know I too feel this must be done, and the sooner the better."

She went on. "There's been talk of restoration, but I reject that idea. The original could never be replicated."

"Hmm," he said, eyebrows raised. "I must say I am rather surprised. I'm curious why you feel that way, considering your own family history with the hotel."

"Indeed, our family does have a proud heritage in the hotel, but that's all memory now. The Swan today is not the Swan of the golden years, when barons and princes mingled with presidents and captains of industry and the queens of society danced to string quartets with men of continental deportment and charm." Suddenly she stiffened and looked around the lobby as muffled strains of *"Folsom Prison Blues"* wafted through the lobby from the old jukebox in the barroom. "Must we suffer that?" she said.

"Pardon?"

"That dreadful noise. My God, when I was a toddler, we had string quartets here, playing Strauss waltzes in the dining room."

Nieman chuckled and gestured to the front-desk clerk to head for the bar and turn down the volume. He grinned, suppressing an urge to keep laughing.

"You find that amusing, young man?"

"Well, that made me think of a Johnny Cash crowd waltzing—just kidding. Go on, please."

"H'mmph. Well, as I was saying, the Swan was once grand, but it's become a decaying relic and an embarrassment to the family and the memories I so cherish. Now it taints our heritage, especially so since the takeover by your company. Of course, the hotel's downward spiral only reflects the disintegration in general of the great cultural strengths of our past."

"Could be, I suppose." He stroked his chin and tried to look serious.

"Those strengths, you understand, are still maintained with vigor by only a few select academic institutions, such as my own. Did I mention Bryn Mawr?"

"Ah, yes. I believe you did," he said.

"Let's not be flippant, Mr. Norman."

"It's Nieman."

"Yes, of course. Now I only mentioned my alma mater because it has enabled its women to become leaders in our world. Men have done nothing but keep the world at war and their women at home and in bed. Pooh. My own memory of men when I was young is that they all just wanted to drink beer and paw all over me. Animals all of them."

"Well, young men are sometimes overly stimulated ... ah, by beautiful women."

"My, my, you do have a clever way with words, Mr. Noonan. Just mind my wishes for the hotel. Now, I wonder if before I go you might call Mr. Handley to the lobby. I'd like a word with him."

"Mr. Handley? Curly? Oh, yes, of course. We seldom use his proper name, but he's probably sleeping right now. He works all night."

"My, what a harsh schedule for such a refined gentleman. So polite and proper—the only one around here who is correct in his manners and in his use of the King's English. In any case, please tell Charles that Sylvia came by to say hello."

"By all means. Feel free to drop by at any time, maybe to talk more about the old days," Nieman said.

"Ah, the old days when a family's name and social standing meant something. But those are all just memories now for an evening's glass of sherry, I suppose. But, must not tarry. I have a meeting of the Junior League to attend."

"Yes, well, it's been so nice of you to come by," he said as they both rose from the lobby chairs.

"Pfff. No one in this town thinks it's nice when I drop by, except my dearest friends. All of them, of course, are from the families like mine who built this town. Of course, we all vote Republican too, you understand."

"Well, of course. Doesn't everyone?" He tried not to smirk.

Chapter 25

Haunting Moment

Boney Pieratt hadn't churned his legs so fast since he ran track at his high school in Kentucky a few decades ago.

A startled guest reading the sports pages of the Plainview Courier in the lobby turned with a jerk that nearly toppled the rocker he sat in as the Swan's maintenance man raced down the stairs, jumped to the landing, and charged across the lobby.

"Mr. Nieman! Mr. Nieman! You better come out here fast as you can. Someone's seen the g-ghost!" he shouted toward he manager's office.

Nieman nearly spilled the cup of coffee he was drinking as a breathless Boney reached the office door.

"This lady's coming down here right now, and boy, is she upset. I never heard n-nobody scream so loud. Like to scared me to death. I was up there replacing light bulbs in the hallway. Like to fell off the ladder."

"Calm down, Boney. There's really no such thing as ghosts," Nieman said.

"Tell her that. The husband said they was staying in the Grant Room, and they was just getting out of b-bed to go get some breakfast, and this young girl started coming at 'em from the wall. I went in the room, while she was still screaming and crying, but I didn't see nothing. I felt my knees getting weak just listenin' to her."

Nieman was suddenly aware of the woman's piercing shrieks as she and her husband came down the stairwell to the lobby.

"What're we gonna do, boss?"

"Play it by ear, Boney." Nieman scratched his chin and then rushed out to the lobby to find his arm clutched by a full-size woman with a terrified look on her face, crying and talking incoherently. Her out-of-breath husband, bags in hand, was trying to comfort her.

"This is Mr. Nieman, the manager, ma'am," said Pieratt. "He'll help out—"

"Oh, this is more than I can take," she said, slumping into a lobby chair, almost pulling Nieman with her, still clinging to his arm and crying uncontrollably.

"I'm so sorry about this, ma'am. Boney, get this lady and her husband some coffee. Maybe that would help."

"I don't think anything will help. Oh, this has unnerved me," she said, sobbing. "It was just about the most frightening thing that's ever happened to me. I can't stop shaking. My husband was just repacking his old uniform — you know, we're going to his old army reunion in Indy. And that thing just started coming at us out of the wall. She was all in blue, a young girl. I thought at first it was a maid. And then I thought maybe I was dreaming—you know, we'd just gotten out of bed—but my husband saw her too. Didn't you, dear?"

Her husband nodded. "Kind of scared me too. We just kept backing up until we'd backed into the other wall, and then she disappeared, kind of gradually till she was gone. Kind of faded away."

A perplexed Nieman assured her the hotel would provide another room. "No charge, of course. I'm so sorry. I'm sure this has been a terrifying experience."

"Oh, I don't think so," said her husband. "I don't think she'll want to stay here at all another night. We both have heart problems, you know."

Calmed, she turned to Nieman. "You know, she was very pretty but young. Wouldn't you say an older teenager, Harold?"

He nodded again. "Light-colored hair … with a white bow on top. She was wearing a long blue dress—yes, sir, light blue with a white collar, like they wore a long time ago. Isn't that right, Helen dear?"

"Yes, she was in blue; the material was very thin, like chiffon," she said, dabbing her eyes with a tissue Nieman had handed her. "You could kind of see right through the dress … and her. That's when I realized it wasn't a real person." She blew her nose and then said, "There was something else too I remember. Did you notice anything odd about her, dear?"

"What?"

"Oh, only a woman would notice, but the way she held her hand over her tummy while she stood there. And that pearl necklace she was holding in the other hand?"

"No, I didn't notice that."

"Harold," she said sharply. "Men are so insensitive. Now I could be wrong, but she certainly looked pregnant to me—not so much so you'd notice it right away but pregnant. And she looked so sad and so very lonely. I felt so sorry for her, and I don't even know why. But it's making me cry all over again."

"Isn't there something we could do to make you feel better about this?" Nieman asked. "Would a glass of sherry be helpful?"

"Oh, no. I don't think so. Come on, Harold; let's look for other accommodations."

"Ahem," uttered her husband timidly. "A refund on the room charge might be helpful."

"Of course," said Nieman, wondering if anyone in the hotel world had ever refunded money for a guest's supernatural experience.

CHAPTER 26

Mysteries Abound

The episode with the ghost was enough to send Nieman back to his office shaking his head and wondering again why fate had brought him to this curious spot in the hotel world. He sat at his desk and played with a Rubik's Cube he'd been given as a fun gift at his going-away party in Atlanta. He'd never figured out the cube's solution. The cryptic penciled note still stuck to his desk drawer seemed a better way to kill a few minutes. He pondered the scribbled letters again: "C h a N T V V s S f i N v." *Change temperature and ventilation? Change the TVs for …? No*, he thought.

He dreamed up some other word combinations but concluded since he wasn't good at solving the Rubik's Cube, the solution to solving the note would probably elude him forever. Or he could save it for whenever he might see Mike Cole again—if he could ever find him. But it was good for a conversation piece in the office.

"Probably meaningless now anyway," he mumbled to no one. His curiosity piqued, he thought instead about a trip to the Swan's cellar to check out the tunnel possibilities. *Might as well have some fun on this job since making the old hotel generate a profit seems to be a hopeless puzzle of its own*, he thought.

He called Faith Quinton at the library. He knew he'd need a better handle on navigating any tunnels he might discover, and she might know where to start.

"You mentioned tunnels when we first met, but you think they've probably been plugged up now, right?" Nieman said.

"I'm not sure. The rumor around town has been that one tunnel starts in what they used to call the coal bin on the east side of the Swan's cellar. That's where I'd start looking. And they say the owner back during Prohibition hid all the expensive wines and liquors stored in one of the tunnels and apparently never went back to retrieve them."

"I wonder why he wouldn't he have gone back."

"Well, I don't know except that the Norton who owned the place then died young, maybe before Prohibition was over, and maybe no one else knew where the stuff was hidden."

"I'll see what I can find, and I'll let you know if it gives me any clues. Thanks again for your help, Faith." He hung up and headed for the library.

CHAPTER 27

Another Look at USG

He held *The Ghosts and Other Legends book* close to the library window to catch the last shaft of light from the late afternoon sun on the yellowing pages. It was a well-worn book. Some pages had come loose from the spine, and the cover's corners were worn with use. That didn't concern Nieman. What did bother him was pencil scribblings he found on a small diagram titled "Plainview's Role in the Underground Railroad System in the Civil War years." Likely some high school student assigned an essay on the fugitive hiding places had spent more time doodling in the book than studying it.

Nieman scanned the book for a while and then focused on a couple of pages on the Swan's tie to the Underground Railroad and a small map. One tunnel stemmed off to the west of the Swan's lobby and led to a residential property. Another angled to the south and appeared to end in the middle of the side yard, under the gazebo. He began copying the map in the steno pad he'd brought along but was startled by Faith Quinton's voice.

"Oh, I see you've come back for more local history."

"Why, hello, Faith. Yes. I had to take a peek at this book you told me about. It's fascinating reading: Indians and Shakers and General Grant and all the other famous people who've been here."

"We're very proud of our town, and personally, I've always been interested in the general in particular."

"Really? I just remember teachers saying his presidency had a lot of problems. I thought he was a drunk, kind of an uncultured oaf, and a generally worthless president with too many scandals."

"That's what a lot of us were taught in school, but when you look closer, his accomplishments are really quite complimentary."

"Hadn't thought much about it."

"I guess you could call me a kind of a Civil War buff," she said, moving her glasses down from the bridge of her nose to look directly over them at him. "But I really got interested in the general because he came here often. And I found he's a very misunderstood man in American history. No one questions he was Lincoln's best general in the war. And then after the war, he favored fairness and leniency instead of punishment for the South's leaders."

She went on. "And when he became president, he fought hard for the Reconstruction program to continue and supported the Fifteenth Amendment so African Americans could vote. And he tried to do all he could while he was in office to help the American Indians in the West. Are you aware that he appointed a Native American as the federal commissioner of Indian Affairs?"

"No, I didn't know that." Nieman was beginning to regret he'd mentioned Grant's name.

"Oh, yes, and you know, we still had the Indians I told you about around here while he was president. Thank

God they hadn't been relocated like so many of our Native Americans in the early days."

Nieman kept listening and nodding and wondering how long she'd go on about Grant.

"But, yes, he did drink a bit of alcohol, but he didn't drink all the time or even regularly. He would drink heavily on occasion, and then for weeks and sometimes months he drank no alcohol. In today's vernacular, he would probably be called a binge drinker.

"He was also skilled writer," she said. "We have his memoirs here. They're beautifully written, and he appreciated good art too, and during the Civil War, he even bought some sketches done by artists who followed the army to battlefields You know, in those days newspapers mostly used artists' sketches of war scenes, but photographers were there too."

"Yes, I've seen a lot of photos of dead Civil War soldiers."

"Well, of course, back then time exposures were the norm," she said. "And dead men don't move. But then I do carry on." She edged slowly toward the door. "I don't want to bore you. I just get so excited talking about the general."

"You aren't boring me," said Nieman, trying hard to sound sincere.

"You know, Grant was a fairly frequent visitor here and often brought his aides with him, probably to play cards with."

"Hmm. I wonder if some of the old newspapers ever wrote about him when he came to town. They'd be interesting to read."

"They certainly would be—and are." She grinned and pointed to the wall behind Nieman. He turned to see a January 1863 front page of the Plainview Courier framed under glass.

Gen. Grant Visits Our City Again During Lull in Vicksburg Battle

Plainview was made proud once again with a visit to our city by the commander of the Union Forces in the West, Gen. Ulysses S. Grant. The *Courier* learned that the general and several aides stayed here last weekend at the Silver Swan and, according to owner August Norton, were shown every courtesy on the three-day visit, which was kept confidential for concerns of military security. They apparently traveled here by train from the south to Louisville, from there by horses provided by the army's supply depot, and finally, by ferryboat across the Ohio. The general stayed in the same second-floor room he has occupied on earlier visits, and his staff all resided on the third floor.

"You know there are families in town who've kept mementos left here by Grant and the officers he traveled with. I've always wondered why no one at the Swan ever finds relics left from those years."

"You mean like souvenirs from the war?"

"Yes."

"Well, I guess I better look in all the closets over there and see if I can find anything." Nieman didn't mention he was already planning to do just that, upstairs and down, but not just in the closets.

Faith left and Nieman retrieved the map he'd stuck in the book and finished his sketch. In a few minutes he closed the book, briskly descended the spiral staircase, and left. For a moment he thought about calling Missy. He wasn't sure why, but he hadn't yet told her about the ghost's appearance, and he'd enjoyed her company on their trip to the recorder's office.

Best to head for the cellar alone first and then ask her to join him over the weekend on a venture to the Swan's antique-filled ballroom, he thought.

CHAPTER 28

Dark Peek at the Past

It was midnight. Handley was doing his usual stint at the front desk, and no late guests were expected. Most of the Swan's residents this night—all nine of them—were likely asleep or watching television shows in their rooms. He started to pull his flask from inside his coat pocket and watch a late-night show on his portable television behind the front desk.

Suddenly, Nieman burst in through the front door. He purposely closed it with a loud bang. Around Handley he'd found it best to make loud entrances after dark, else find him asleep on the job, and then he'd be forced to bawl him out or fire him.

"Good evening, sir." Handley let the flask drop back into his pocket and tried to look busy with the guest register.

"I've got to check the telephone lines in the basement," Nieman told the startled night auditor as he walked to the basement door. "Some guests have been complaining." He didn't know anything about phone lines, but he knew Handley would probably fall asleep on the job shortly anyway and wouldn't need an explanation. He had to see any tunnel for himself, if there was one, and also see if it was blocked, as Faith said she suspected for years. It compelled a foray into the dark and smelly cellar.

Nieman was expecting to see an unpleasant place, and he wasn't disappointed. As he descended the creaking wooden steps, he thought about the kind of cellar Dorothy would have run to when a tornado was spotted on the western Kansas horizon.

Clutching his hand-drawn map, he switched on the lights. There were six incandescent bulbs swinging from wiring nailed to floor joist timbers resting on the soot-blackened concrete walls. He imagined a dungeon in the Dark Ages. Boney Pieratt's description as "just a nasty place" surely fit.

Even with the lights on, Nieman could barely see the floor. He kept his head down for fear of bumping against the low timber joists above him. Squinting in the darkness, he could see a low door he guessed might lead to the coal bin, which probably hadn't been used since the world converted to natural gas back in the 1940s.

Nieman was glad he'd worn gloves, as he found himself sweeping away decades of the webbed artwork of countless spiders, dead and alive, hanging from the floor timbers. He squeezed his body around the decades-old soot-streaked stoker that once moved coal on a conveyor to the furnace and reached the small door to the coal bin, where the map in the library book had shown an access to a tunnel.

Once inside, he put the beam of his flashlight on walls blackened from decades of coal dumped in through an outside chute. Concrete blocks showing no mortar formed one wall he judged to be about five feet high. He could see the tips of rebar had been inserted in the blocks from top to bottom to prevent casual removal by curious employees. He hoped the wall hid a tunnel entrance.

Slowly, he muscled the end of a top end-block to pivot it outward. Adrenalin flowing now, he tugged at lower blocks, and with them came handfuls of loose dirt cascading down on him from the earthen entrance. He got a mouthful and coughed, wondering how much old coal dust he'd inhaled.

The opening was big enough now, and he managed to squeeze his head and shoulders between the blocks and the dirt wall and peered into the darkness. Directing the beam of his flashlight into the black void, he could see several wine bottles overturned on the dirt floor. They were empty, and he could only see part of the labels. But he'd seen enough. The wines were old—late-1800s old —and French. And they would have fetched high bids from collectors. How many more might lie beyond his reach in the darkness?

Curiosity aroused, for a moment he thought about getting all the way into the dark hole to go farther into the tunnel. But he remembered his promise to Missy, to take her to the Swan's old ballroom tomorrow. The tunnel would have to wait. Right now what he really wanted was to wash off all that Indiana dirt. He backed out and headed upstairs to the carriage house.

Chapter 29

Antique Heaven

Nieman put his shoulder against the tall walnut cabinet that blocked the double doors of the old ballroom and pushed hard. It didn't budge.

"Let me help," said Missy, moving across the fourth-floor landing to Nieman's side. Together they moved the cabinet a few inches away from the doors. Nieman stuck his head through the partial opening.

"Wow. A real jumble of stuff. Chairs and tables heaped on top of more chairs and tables, and God knows what is piled everywhere, nearly to the ceiling. I don't know how we'll ever get through it all."

They shoved the cabinet a few more inches and finally managed to squeeze their bodies through the half-opened door.

"I see what you mean," she said, looking around the half-dark ballroom, the only light coming from the morning sun poking through shuttered dormer windows.

Nieman scratched his head, trying to figure out the easiest way to navigate the sea of old furniture and other dusty reminders of the past sprawled across the jammed floor. He leaned against a large ornately carved armoire and shoved it aside to open a path of sorts. The two moved across the room slowly, careful to avoid tripping on packing boxes scattered around the floor.

The doors on some cabinets stood open, one revealing porcelain tableware, creamers, and small finger bowls. Another held a large samovar he guessed was sterling. He pointed it out to Missy, who trailed him by a few feet.

Framed artwork, statuary, lamp tables, and dressers, some with open drawers stuffed with hotel bric-a-brac, had been stored randomly over what was once a polished dance floor where well-heeled guests partied. He paused to study several paintings in sculpted gilt frames leaning against the wall. He'd seen prints of some before, but these were on canvas. One, a Bierstadt, looked original. *More likely*, he thought, *just a reproduction*.

He turned to show Missy, but she was bending down a few feet away, looking for the manufacturer's label on a small writing desk.

He backed up to take a better look at the artwork but stumbled into a stack of what he thought were cooking pans. They hit the hardwood floor with a metallic crash.

"What was that?" shouted a startled Missy.

"Pretty funny, actually. Look." Nieman laughed, holding up one of the "pans" so she could see it.

"Brass spittoons—that is, cuspidors. Talk of your social incorrectness today. But these babies were used when men were men."

"Yeeck. They were disgusting back then," she said, "and now, I might add."

They both giggled and went on exploring amid the sea of discards.

"A heck of a lot of old stuff up here, but some high-value stuff too," Missy said as they maneuvered across the ballroom's dance floor. "I bet that cherry armoire we saw back there would fetch a few thousand, and there's another here just like it."

"It's obvious," said Nieman, "some long-ago managers just threw the used stuff up here whenever the owners brought new things in from Chicago, or maybe even Europe." He talked as he edged around a tall glass-front china cabinet full of Victorian silverware wrapped in cloth, ceramic figurines, and crystal. "You still back there?" he shouted as he wedged his way through the assortment of long-forgotten hostelry furnishings.

Missy lingered. In the low light she was straining to read labels on furniture. "Yes. I'm still here. A lot of these things look to be pre-Civil War."

"Really?"

"I think so. I'm no antique expert, but some of these chairs back here and a settee are Chippendale, and they're obviously ancient, probably originals and still beautiful."

"They just look worn and old to me."

"Antique traders will pay big money for some of these things. See this?" She kneeled down, looking for a trademark. "This is a corner server, and the name looks like Roycraft. That's a name I've heard in antiques." She climbed over an upended, marble-top side table and grabbed a chair next to it, with a needle-worked upholstered seat. "This is Queen Anne. Worth a lot if it's authentic. There were a lot of Queen Anne reproductions, but I've been told even some of those have antique value now."

"I guess the Nortons really did know the right stuff to buy," said Nieman, now on his knees under a large table he judged to be cherry. "This one was made in England."

Missy pointed to a large chest on the floor. "This looks like a Shaker blanket chest. And most of these chairs are Shaker too. Wonder why they'd have Shaker stuff—not very fancy."

"Faith told me they used to have a local colony here," said Nieman as he tried to move a steamer chest out of his way. It was too heavy. He lifted the lid. "Hey, this is full of what looks Wedgwood. We had some for special guests at the Grande Arms."

He moved to the front of the ballroom, where a piano under a dust cover stood on a riser.

"It's a Steinway. Gotta be real old, and you know they usually appreciate with age. I remember seeing it listed as just 'an old grand piano' in the company inventory."

A crumpled yellowed paper on the floor caught Missy's eye. She picked it up and unfolded it. An entry in the 1927 concert program read: "*The Trout*, a quintet by Franz Shubert, to be performed by ..." She pondered it for a few minutes, envisioning the fashionable crowd that once would have been seated in what was now a dim and dusty storage place with only reminders of that long-ago time.

"You had enough for the day?" Nieman asked. "Let's get out of all this dust and get some fresh air for a change."

"Okay, let's call it quits for now," she said, turning toward the door. "We can always come back."

"By the way," said Nieman as the two worked their way back to the stairway landing, "you still willing to go down in the cellar with me and Boney to see what's there? Probably won't be any antiques, but maybe the owners stashed some other goodies down there, like old wines."

"That'd be fun, Mr. Innkeeper," she said. "Now, how about being a gentleman and giving me your hand, so I don't trip going down these steep steps. After all, I don't want to sue the Swan for a fall on an unsafe stairway, do I?"

"Very cute, Madam Attorney. No, we wouldn't want that," he said as he took her hand and pressed it firmly. "Now, remember, if you're going with us this weekend, don't wear those three-inch heels you wear in court to impress the boys in the jury. Believe me, the cellar's no place for a fashion statement."

Chapter 30

A Search for the Past

Very carefully, as if moving the wrong concrete block might collapse the rear of the building, Nieman loosened the end of the top end block, pivoting it out just as he had on his first venture to the musty coal bin. Behind him, Missy and Boney aimed flashlights at the wall as he pulled out the ends of some lower end blocks, just enough to give him space to squeeze through the opening.

"Whew," he said. "I feel like that guy who opened up King Tut's tomb."

"Yeah," said Missy, "but he was looking for gold and diamonds and mummies. I have a feeling we're not going to find anything here more than just plain dirt. Tell me again why we're here."

"Ask me later." Nieman crawled through and Missy followed, not without grumbling about getting her slacks dirty. They stood waving their flashlights around and staring into the black tunnel behind the wall, leaving Boney alone still in the coal bin.

Nieman looked down to retrieve the empty bottle he'd spotted on his first look behind the wall and tossed it aside.

"This is kind of exciting. I guess it's just the fun of exploration."

"Some fun," said Missy. "To me it's just creepy. But let's not forget Boney. He's probably gone back upstairs by now."

Nieman shouted toward the opening. "Hey, Boney. C'mon. You're skinny enough to get through there without touching any dirt." They could hear him muttering to himself as he wedged himself through the crevice to join them.

"Mr. Lee, this … this place looks jes' like one of them old dungeons where they kept prisoners in chains and tortured 'em. You sure nothin's going to fall on us? This is m-makin' me all nervous."

"Relax, Boney. Nothing's going to fall on us. This tunnel's been here for decades."

"I just wanta g-get outta here. It's makin' my knees give out."

"You'll be okay. Let's just do it." Nieman grabbed Missy's arm, and all three bent low and slowly moved deeper into the tunnel, careful not to stumble on the rough earthen floor.

They found themselves looking into a blackness thick with spider webs and tree roots poking through the dirt walls, the air damp and foul all around.

Boney tripped and fell on something lying on the ground. "I'm shaking, boss. This place is too scary." He groaned as he got back up.

"I'd have to agree with that," said Missy, her voice muffled by the surrounding earth. "This place is giving me the creeps too. All these spider webs and worms and creepy bugs crawling around—yeeck."

"Hang with me, people," Nieman said, trying to sound in charge. He directed his flashlight beam on the ground to see what had tripped up Boney. He picked up two dirt-caked, empty wine bottles and looked closely at the labels.

One label showed a sketch of a Victorian mansion behind the words "Chateau Haut-Brion" and "Graves." The other showed a printed signature: "Philippe Rothschild 1939."

"Were they good years?" asked Missy as the three moved deeper into the tunnel, bending even lower now to avoid the dirt ceiling and spider webs as the tunnel narrowed.

"I don't know. We'll have to ask Curly. He worked as a sommelier a long time ago. I just hope we can find a few with something in them. That'd be more exciting."

"Yeah, but I'd rather be upstairs drinking them than what we're doing. That sounds more exciting to me."

"Me too, but don't give up on me now. There could be more down here. Curly told me that red wines stand up best to time and could be valuable. People who go to wine auctions like the thrill of the risk. Some old wines turn to vinegar, but they don't know that until they uncork them."

They moved without talking, into the blackness. Missy broke the silence. "I wonder if any fugitive slaves ever really hid down here?"

"Faith said they did. Fugitive slaves would be hidden in places like this overnight, until they could go to some other safe place."

"I'd sure like to go to some safer place right now too, boss, one with lights." Boney's voice was shaking now.

"I know you would, Boney, but—hey, wait a second." Nieman spotted an opening in the dirt at the top of one side of the tunnel. "Let's see if there's anything on the other side. Boney, let me lift you up there."

"I jes' as soon not do that, if you don't mind, Mr. Lee. All I want to do is g-get outta here."

"Here, I'll take a look," said Missy, moving to the side and pocketing her flashlight. "Where's the opening?"

"Put your light on it up there, Boney." Nieman gripped his fingers together on both hands, motioning to Missy to put her foot on his cupped fingers, so she could get up to look over the dirt wall.

"See anything?" asked Nieman, handing her his flashlight.

"Not yet. Wait till I get my head at the right angle and get these awful spider webs out of my face. I'm not anxious to be doing this, you know."

Several minutes passed in silence.

"You see anything yet?" he asked again

"Don't rush me, mister. Remember, I'm a volunteer on this job. There's really nothing there. Just a lot of rubble and debris … and some empty bottles … not much, really."

Nieman was disappointed. He'd hoped for a better answer. But he sensed Missy had seen more as he lowered her to the ground. Maybe she'd seen a skeleton, or maybe he'd watched too many TV shows about paranormal hauntings. He'd ask her later.

Missy brushed off her jacket. "Let's get out of here."

"Not yet. Come on. Let's follow the passageway to the south now and see if we find anything else. If I'm right, this will go out under the yard another twenty feet or so, to the gazebo and wishing pond, before it turns in another direction."

"Where's Boney?" said Nieman, flashing his light behind Missy.

"He's gone," she said, chuckling. "Said he was shaking like a 'virgin on the verge' and left. Frankly, Lee, I'd like to get out of here too."

"All right, I give. But I can't stop. It's like being a Boy Scout again, exploring the woods in back of your house."

"Maybe that's why there were Boy Scouts before there were Girl Scouts. Personally, I'd rather be exploring a cold soda."

"Okay, but before you go, what'd you really see back there?"

"Well," she said, "I thought it best not to let Boney know, or it'd be all over town. It looked like a storage place for wines and whiskeys, cases of both. Some of the wine cases were marked in French. I bet it was all hidden there when Prohibition came along."

"You're probably right. Somebody took all the good stuff from the wine cellar at the hotel and hid it all here."

"Maybe, but whoever did it wouldn't have forgotten about it."

"No," said Nieman, "but Faith told me that one of the Nortons died young in the 1930s, maybe before Prohibition ended, and no one else knew all this was down here. Anyway, why not come with me farther back?"

"No, thanks." She brushed back hair from her forehead with the back of her hand. "A hot bath looks better to me right now. Explore away on your own, scout leader. Boney had the right idea. See you upstairs."

Chapter 31

A Deeper Look Pays Off

Alone now on his hands and knees, Nieman crawled farther back in the narrowing tunnel. He paused for a moment to focus the glow of his flashlight on the penciled map he'd brought along. "Maybe another fifty feet," he said in the blackness.

But there was a problem. A high pile of earth and rocks blocked the passage. Crawling to the top of the mound, he began clawing the dirt and stones back until he'd opened a gap and crawled through. He came to a widening and stumbled on what looked to him like a packet of papers. Looking closely, he could see they were deteriorating newspaper pages and documents all bound in a leather binder. He could read part of a faded headline and battlefield sketch on a partly disintegrated page of a Louisville newspaper dated 1862: "Grant Takes Fort on Tennessee River."

Nieman grabbed the straps around the packet and dragged it behind him. Swiping his light to the other side of the opening, he found himself looking at an assortment of decaying and mold-covered objects randomly scattered on the ground. Only the frames remained of two folding chairs and a cot, the canvas rotted away. A small, portable desk stood silent nearby, and some military apparel and blankets lay in a crumpled pile in the dirt.

Several rifles stood in a stack in a crevice in the earthen wall. Nieman knew firearms. These weren't muzzle loaders that most soldiers used in the Civil War. He grabbed the moldy leather strap on one and dragged the rifle behind him, along with the packet of papers, and crawled to the other side of the opening, where he saw a dark wooden box. Opening it, he found two percussion pistols and two newer revolvers inside, one in a molded leather holster engraved with the initials USG. He could see the word *Colt* on one pistol. Another was stamped with the letters *CS*. He tucked it in a pocket.

By the other dirt wall, Nieman could see wine bottles lying around, one a French cognac with the label dated 1871. It was empty, but two others weren't. He took off his belt, lashed the two together, and crawled away, pulling them behind him, along with the papers and rifle, hoping the bottles wouldn't break as he moved away.

Nieman didn't go far. A rotting canvas bag on the ground caught his eye. Covered with mold, insect droppings, and spider webs, it was partly deteriorated. As he pulled the rope-laced opening apart, he found himself gagging from the foul odor coming out of the bag. "Phew!" he said in the darkness.

When Nieman looked inside with the now-dim illumination of his flashlight, he found himself looking at a tangled mess of leather straps and feathers. He guessed it was the work of a taxidermist, maybe a mounted wild turkey or some other bird-hunting trophy of a kill taken by some nineteenth-century sportsman. Or maybe it was just a discarded costume from a long-ago masquerade ball. He held his breath, quickly closed the top, and moved away from the smelly package.

As Nieman retraced his way out, his foot kicked some metal objects on the ground. He looked down to see three swords, two rusted together but one in a sheath that appeared to be in better condition. He was reminded of a brief session he'd had with bayonets in boot camp at Fort Leonard Wood and wondered if Union soldiers ever practiced with swords. He couldn't resist the temptation and picked up the sheathed sword; he hooked the handguard onto a belt loop on his trousers and crawled away with his growing load of relics in tow.

Resting on the dirt floor for a moment, the Swan manager sat in wonderment at what he had seen. But his batteries were almost dead now, and he needed fresh air. On hands and knees, he headed back to the Swan's cellar, a labored foot or so at a time, the revolver still in his jacket pocket and still dragging his other booty behind him across the tunnel floor.

Nobody is going to believe all this, he thought as he stumbled into the dark hotel cellar and climbed the stairs to the lobby, lugging the rewards of his underground expedition behind him.

Scuffed up and dirty, Nieman opened the cellar door to the lobby as inconspicuously as he could and hoped Handley would be sleeping on the job by now.

It wasn't to be. A startled Handley, still on the job at the front desk, looked at him with raised eyebrows. "Well, sir, looks like you've been on a bit of an expedition."

"Good evening, Curly. Any business tonight?" he asked, trying to change the subject. But with all the gear he dropped on the lobby floor, Handley was mesmerized with curiosity. Nieman grabbed up the two bottles of wine and untied the belt tying them together.

"Sir, begging your pardon, you look like a man who's just survived trench warfare. Might I ask what you're holding in your hand?"

Nieman gave up on any clandestine feint and held up the two bottles. "Handley, my man, I've been exploring the basement. All sorts of things down there, if you look hard enough."

Handley took a closer look at the labels on the bottles. "By God, sir. This place hasn't seen the likes of that in our lifetimes."

"What do you mean? Just because they're old?" asked Nieman, putting the bottles on the counter top.

"Yes, but more so the year, the appellation," he said, studying the label. "I might say, sir, if the crew on the Titanic thought the lounge bar stocked a few bottles of Romanée-Conti like these, they would never have abandoned ship."

Nieman chuckled but decided this wasn't the right moment to elaborate on his venture. "I'll tell you about all this stuff later, my man. But right now I'm going to hide all this stuff in a closet. I need a good hot shower." He headed to the carriage house.

"Indeed, indeed," Handley said as he continued to stare in wonder at the lobby floor even after his boss left.

Chapter 32

Summing Up

"All this history is going to make me thirsty," Missy said, almost in a whisper. She and Nieman sat in his apartment, where he had stashed the finds from his extended excursion.

"Just thought you should see the stuff I found. Remember what they say about those who ignore history?"

"I'm not ignoring history, but do you have anything to drink here besides spoiled milk and old wines too risky to swallow? After all, I am your guest."

"Forgot my manners. Yes, there's some unspoiled ginger ale and maybe a Coke in the fridge. Sorry, I don't have anything stronger on tap. I don't entertain here very often."

"I'll bet," she said as she headed for the kitchen. "You've probably already spoiled a few local women up here."

"No, no. It's all been strictly work ... so far at least." He rose and pulled the rifle and sword from a closet.

"Whoa!" she said as she returned. "You planning to kill me now that I know where you put all these things?"

"No, not right away." He chuckled. "But since our journey the other day, I've done a little research. This is a Henry rifle. There were two others down there. From what I've read, they were the first repeating rifles used in the Civil War. We're talking big money here to collectors. But I haven't found anything on the sword yet."

"All this does make a person feel kind of strange, doesn't it?" she said. "All these things that no one has seen for, what, a hundred years or more, and a lot is high value now. All those antiques in the ballroom would be worth a fortune to collectors, Lee. I can't imagine what today's values would be on that initialed Wedgwood matched pitcher and sugar bowl set—or those Canton dishes that look so ordinary or that Sheffield silver-plate punch bowl."

"And there are all the wines I've been bringing up for Handley to keep track of."

"But is he counting them or drinking them?" she asked.

"No, he's doing a good job of putting a value on them. But you know, it's ironic. We have all this valuable stuff around here, but that wouldn't help a person who might want to buy the place and didn't have enough money."

"I suppose, but you're not thinking about buying it, are you?"

"Well, the thought has crossed my mind, kind of."

"I'm not surprised, but I wasn't talking about just the money values here. Finding all these old things gives you a different perspective. It feels odd, like you're part of the history you're looking at."

"It does," Nieman said.

"It makes me think of all the people who used to come here," she said, sipping her ginger ale. "In your imagination you can almost see them walking around: Grant playing cards with his staff and talking about the war, James Whitcomb Riley having a drink and then writing a poem, P. T. Barnum planning his circus's next gig, Dickens looking out the window and wondering how the rhubarbs in America ever made it this far as a democracy."

"It does make you think about life and how things don't really change much. There are still rifles and wars, still circuses and circus owners, and still poets."

"They're just not staying at the Swan very often now," Missy said.

"Back in Atlanta, an old guy who used to stay at the Grande Arms told me once, 'If you think things change, you haven't lived long enough, son.' Good way to look at life, huh?"

"Could be, innkeeper. I'll let you know for sure when I'm old enough to think about it."

The two laughed and then looked at each other for a few moments without speaking as the sunlight coming through the apartment windows faded with dusk and the room darkened.

"Seriously," he said, "what bothers me about finding all these things here is that all they all came from beneath that land owned by that Indian tribe. So, maybe it's not ours and maybe not the hotel's either." Seated in a chair opposite Missy on the couch, he took her hands in his. "Look, I've done a lot of thinking lately. Maybe I could buy the place and make a go of it. Maybe."

"Wow. That's certainly ambitious," she said.

"I think I might be able to find a few people to invest some money for part of a down payment, but I'm not sure how I could afford the rest or even more to operate it, get it rolling, and then restore it. That'd take a lot more."

"You can't buy it if you're working for the company that owns it."

"I could quit and then make an offer. But I'd need your help," he said, still holding her hands, but tighter now. "Will you help me do this?" They leaned together closer as they sat. "I mean, I don't want to run into any legal problems … plus I just want you with me. Know what I mean?"

He kissed her. She didn't pull back. She smiled, and with a lilt in her voice, she whispered in the quiet of the room,

"Naturally I'll help. Only because it's you, though, because I do think it's a pretty dicey risk."

"You mean that?"

"Yes, because it's you. And I like a challenge."

He stood and pulled her up from the couch. He put his arms around her, and they kissed again for a long few seconds.

"I'm not going to be your problem, mister," she said in a hushed voice. "But straightening out ownership of this property for a mortgage will be, not to mention finding more money."

"They say everything comes in threes. I got divorced and demoted and then sent out here. Now, it's money, finding a lost Indian, and talking an old spinster into something she doesn't want to do."

"I'll help, but I can't negotiate with a maybe-dead Indian, and I certainly don't want to deal with old Sylvia. The last time I ran into her she told me for the umpteenth time I should have gone to an Ivy League law school instead of IU. But right now I better get out of here before—like a good bachelor—you talk me into staying the night."

"Would I do that?" he said, grinning.

"Oh, yes, I think so."

They kissed again, this time longer, and before she could open the door, he said, "Hey, I've got something else to show you at the hotel. Why don't you drop by sometime tomorrow?"

"Okay, bye now."

"But don't come too early," he yelled down the carriage house steps. "Boney and I are going to paint the lobby in the morning, to start getting the place freshened up."

He watched her as she crossed the hotel lawn. He hadn't had these kinds of stirrings since he met his now ex-wife on the Emory campus twenty years ago. Clearly, his life was taking some curious twists since his arrival at Indiana's most legendary, if not most neglected, lodging establishment.

Chapter 33

The Mayor Gives a Nod

Nieman and his maintenance man had just finished painting one wall of the lobby and admiring their work when Mayor Gomia burst through the Swan's front door.

"Howdy, gentlemen," he said in his usual spirited political manner.

"Hello, Mr. Mayor," Nieman called down from the ladder he stood on. "What brings you to our humble house of hospitality?"

Gomia looked up at the wall. "Sure does look brighter in here, brighter than it's been for years. Lookin' good, gentlemen."

"We're trying to get the whole place looking better."

"About time somebody's doing something with this old lady, yes, sir. I dropped by for a couple of reasons. One, I wanted you to hear the good news we got at city hall. The state's given us approval to change the name of the town to Grantville."

"That sounds great. Congratulations." Nieman stepped down from the ladder and extended his hand to Gomia. Boney gestured to the mayor with a thumbs-up as he put the lid back on a can of soft-yellow paint.

"Well, thank you both. Appreciate that. Course it's not official until January, but we're tickled pink about it down at city hall, and I'm just spreading the word around town."

Nieman breathed easier. He'd worried the mayor had come about the rusted second-floor fire escape problem.

"Well, I'm headed to the Rotary luncheon, and I'd like to tell 'em what you're planning to do with this place. The town's really concerned, you know."

"Ah, I wasn't sure earlier what was going to happen. But now I think I have a better handle on it, maybe." Nieman was cleaning his paint-spattered hands with a rag. "I think what's going to happen is I'm leaving the company and making an offer to buy the place myself … maybe."

"Son of a gun," said Gomia. "I think that'd be great. Everybody'd love to have local ownership. Proud of you, son. If you don't mind my asking, how you gonna finance it?"

"I think I'll form a company and look for seed money. I think after we get it all cleaned up, we can draw more business, and then someday down the road, maybe restore the whole place."

"That'd be just wonderful. Can I tell the boys at the Rotary meeting today?"

"Sure, but tell them this is all tentative right now. I've got a lot planning to do, like figuring out a business plan for the bank. I'll keep you posted on how it's going."

"You know, son, I just might be interested myself in getting in on it a little, and you know the city might have one of our new economic incentive programs that could help you out too."

"It sure would help," said a smiling Nieman.

Gomia paused and looked up at the newly painted wall. "Yes, sir, when I see the boss working along with his employees and getting his hands dirty, I say there's a man who has spunk, a man who knows how to win loyalty and turn work into money.

By God, it's just like pickin' cotton, getting all hands working together. You know what I mean?"

"Sure do," said Nieman, trying to hide his excitement. "But there are a couple of hurdles we'll have to jump to get the bank to move on this." He told Gomia about Sylvia Norton's ties to the Swan, as well as the Indian puzzle.

"Indians? You kidding me?"

"No. Their name's still on the deed. It's a long story," said Nieman, glancing at his watch. "I'll tell you about it someday when I have more time. But I'll tell you this: the Indian I'm talking about is older than Sylvia, and for some reason he's been on the war path with the Swan for a long time."

"Well, I'll be hog-tied. I don't know how I can help you with that, and Sylvia's a tough old bird. You gotta lean on her heritage. Tell her a new Swan can extend her family name into the future."

"Good advice. She is a bit of a glitch in the plan."

"Well, I hope you can work it out, but right now I gotta head to the Rotary meeting. Oh, by the way, you think the new name will get us on the map, so to speak?"

"Oh, I think it's a great move. It's marketable, and the town'll get more recognition. Companies doing business here should love it."

"That's what I been saying all along," said Gomia as he left.

Nieman headed to his office, flush with the possibility of at least one potential investor besides himself.

Chapter 34

Cutting the Tie?

Nieman looked up from his phone as Missy knocked softly and poked her head through the half-open door to his office.

"Can I come in?" she mouthed. He waved her in and pointed to a chair. He cupped his mouth and whispered, "I'm calling my boss at the home office. I'm on speaker phone."

"Hello, Bob? This is Lee in Indiana."

"Hey, how's our Hoosier doing these days. Still losing money?" Prestik said.

"We're getting a few more people in here these days, just a few more. I put an ad in Indiana's AAA magazine, and we're cleaning up the place a little. Bu that's not what I'm calling about."

"Oh?" The mood suddenly got more serious. "So, what's up?"

"Well, ah, you know how I told you the last time we talked that I was getting comfortable here? Well, you'll probably think I'm balmy, but I'm thinking about quitting, buying the place myself, and making a go of it."

"Wow, you're shocking me, Lee."

"I know. But don't turn in my resignation yet. There are some things I have to figure out first."

"Am I hearing you right? You know they're asking four and a quarter. You'd be taking a huge risk. The Swan's best days were over a long time ago, Lee. Even your predecessor had a hard time paying the bills. You know that."

"I know, but I think in time I could turn it around. I even think I've found my first investor."

"Whew. I'm still kind of shocked, but I know you've got a good business head. I'll go ahead and tell the CEO what you're thinking about doing, and we'll see how he reacts. Okay?"

"Okay, pal. Just wish me luck. I'll keep you posted if I can make an offer."

Nieman put down the phone, and he and Missy looked at each other.

"Well, you did it. Scared?" Missy asked.

"Yeah, a little. I don't know how I'll come up with enough money. And then Then there's the Sylvia Norton thing and the Indian quirk in the deed. But, you know, I'm having a good feeling about it. I've got the kitchen crew cleaning up the equipment, and I gave them some ideas on a new menu—something more than just hamburgers and fries. Our bartender's going to trade school, so he'll be able to mix more than a shot and Coke. Hey, I've even taught Boney how to adjust the flush valve on a toilet."

"Oh, Lee, you're really a good boss. These people would almost work for you for free."

"I wish they would," he said. "Oh, I almost forgot something." He jumped up and reached for a packet of papers by his desk.

Chapter 35

Forgot to Mail It?

The packet held the documents he'd found along with the rifles and other booty on his extended underground venture.

"I finally opened it all the way and read some of the documents. They're really amazing."

"Don't you feel like you're opening the Dead Sea Scrolls?"

"Yes, kind of." He cautiously lifted the leather cover from the top sheet, a faded and partly deteriorated front page of a Louisville newspaper dated February 20, 1862.

Grant's Forces Take Fort Donelson

Some three thousand Confederate soldiers managed to escape, but the Union forces claim they were able to capture some fifteen thousand men when Fort Donelson capitulated in recent days.

Union officers told the newspaper journalists on the scene that this was a significant victory for Grant, since the fort had stood as the citadel of protection for the lower Cumberland River.

"God," she said. "This is really is exciting stuff to read." She was wide-eyed as he separated another partly missing sheet from the packet.

"Sure is. Look at this." He stopped short and then stared at a small sheet of stationary stamped with "US Government" at the top.

"Wow!" Missy shouted as they found themselves looking at what was a handwritten letter, *to the president*. "Was this to Lincoln?"

Dear Mr. President:

I deeply appreciate your analysis of the maneuvers at Vicksburg. As you obviously understand, we faced a number of obstacles, not the least being the river itself, and the high terrain on which the Confederate forces were positioned—not to mention their fierce desire to defend the city that holds the power to control river traffic.

We felt that our plan, which to be very honest was not a sure thing, seemed to be about the best option, based on our lack of success with other approaches.

But in the end, victory was ours, fortunately, and I was very proud of the manner in which our troops—and those of the naval forces as well—performed their duties.

I have taken the liberty of informing my commanders of your gracious appreciation of our strategy, so that they may in turn tell their various troop elements we have well served our nation and the righteous cause of the Union.

Thank you so much for your gracious and insightful remarks.

Very respectively yours,
USG

Nieman and Missy continued to stare at the letter, and then they looked at each other. She said, "You have to wonder why this was never sent to Washington. Or maybe this was a first draft and Grant wasn't satisfied with it."

"We should send this to some Civil War expert or maybe to my old history professor at Emory, if he's still around. He'll know where it fits into history. Frankly, I'm dumbstruck."

"Me too. This whole thing has been beyond belief, hasn't it?"

"It has been, but this letter is really valuable. We could sell it and put the proceeds into more down payment on the Swan."

"Oh, Lee, you can't do that with this kind of thing. It's too important to sell. It really should go to a museum, like the Smithsonian, or we'd both feel guilty for not sharing it with the public."

"I guess you're right. Besides, like the wines Curly's keeping track of, these came from under the land that Indian tribe still owns, I guess. Anyway," he said, putting the papers down, "maybe it's time to sit down, have a drink, and think about all this. Our bartender should be able by now to mix a margarita for you, and if he can't, I'll give him a quick lesson."

He grabbed her hand, kissed her on the cheek, and led her to the Swan's barroom. "You know, that Grant letter—maybe he just forgot to mail it."

They giggled over the remark as they walked down the hallway holding hands.

"It's strange," said Missy. "I'm beginning to feel like Scarlett O'Hara with all this Civil War business: the rifles, the sword, the letter."

"History does that for you."

"Yes, but Rhett Butler would have kissed me longer," she said, feigning a pout and pressing against him as they walked down the hallway.

"I was just trying you out," he said, putting his arm around her shoulders. "Next time I'll buckle on the sword and do a more gentlemanly job of it."

"I accept your proposition, sir," she said. "But considering the occasion, you should teach your barkeep one other drink before the South rises again. How about a mint julep?"

"Wrong season but sounds good to me," he said, kissing her ear as they reached the bar. "But just remember: Frankly, my dear, I do give a damn."

"Oh, there you are," the bartender said as they stepped into the nearly deserted room. "You got a call up front, Mr. Nieman … from Miss Quinton. They called on the intercom."

"Wonder what Faith wants. Let's do the mint julep later. Okay?"

"I guess so. Too early to drink anyway, and I have to get back to work. Can't just play all the time, can we?"

"No, but I'd like to," he said, and they left, arms around each other and the bartender all eyes.

Chapter 36

Finding Indian Joe

Nieman waved to Missy, walked into his office, and picked up the phone.

"Hello, Faith, what can I do for you?"

"Well, Mr. Nieman, I may have some good news for you."

"Oh, really?"

"You know, I have birding friends all over Indiana. We stay in contact in case we have an unusual sighting of birds we don't ordinarily see in our own areas of the state."

"I see. Please go on." Nieman suddenly regretted appearing too enthusiastic about the bird world when he visited Faith.

"Well, it just so happens I have a birding friend in Indianapolis, to whom I mentioned on the phone something about your search for a lost Indian. And don't you know, she popped right up and said, 'There's one right here downtown. Been here for years, a homeless guy.'"

"Son of a gun," said Nieman. "I wonder—"

"Oh, I know what you're thinking," she said, breaking in. "Here's where this gets to be good news and bad news, I think."

"How so?"

"My friend went right downtown and talked to the man. It turned out he's one of those who hangs around downtown, begging for a handout."

"Really?"

"Yes, and he said he used to live in Plainview, but when my friend said someone at the Silver Swan was looking for him, his whole attitude changed. She said he started grumbling about the hotel and the old days."

"Hmm."

"He told her he was definitely not interested in talking with anyone connected with the Swan."

"You have to wonder why."

"You do."

"Did she give you a name?"

"She said everybody downtown calls him "Indian Joe," but some of the other homeless people around him said he also goes by the name of 'Eagle' something too, but she didn't understand the name exactly."

Faith went on. "Now, what sets him apart is that all day long he pounds on a drum he carries around, and he chants and tells people about how badly the Indians were treated years ago. He told her he was ninety-five years old and is the last living member of his tribe—the tribe that used to live here."

"I'll be darned," said Nieman. "Boy, I gotta meet this guy. He sounds like the right Indian to talk to about that piece of land here."

"He might not want to talk to you, Mr. Nieman, but my friend said he's down at Monument Circle every day."

"I've been told that Indians don't show their emotions much, but I think I could lighten him up and figure out why he doesn't like the Swan. Maybe we could have a friendly sit-down." Nieman chuckled.

"I hope you can too, but please call me if you go up there. It'd be exciting to tell the historical society all about it. Bye now."

Chapter 37

An Indian Viewpoint

As he drove to Indianapolis, Nieman thought about what he'd say to the Indian and why a man who hadn't been in town for years could still harbor a grudge against the hotel. Maybe management somehow insulted him a long time ago. Maybe it was a matter of discrimination.

After asking a pedestrians for directions, he pulled into a parking garage near the landmark Monument Circle in the heart of Indy's downtown. He walked toward the tall Soldiers' and Sailors' Monument topped by a statue of what he'd been told was Lady Victory. He looked up but could barely see her; he was too close. But he could hear the soft drumbeat Faith's friend had mentioned, and as he got closer to the sound, he could see the Indian chanting and thumping on what looked like a handcrafted tom-tom.

His jeans were threadbare and worn through at the knees. A long feather dangled from the rim of a crushed, black porkpie hat that contrasted with the mass of mostly gray hair hanging down his back in a ponytail.

Nieman walked up and extended his hand. "Hello. My name is Nieman, and I've come from Plainview to talk with you, if you don't mind, Mr., ah, Eagle?"

The Indian did not reciprocate with a handshake but glared at Nieman, brows furrowed on a chiseled leathery face. "It's Eagleman, and if you are employed by the Silver Swan, as I suspect, I have no interest in talking further."

"I understand, but—"

"I'm afraid, young man, that you don't understand," the Indian replied, cutting him off.

A young boy dropped two quarters into the tin cup on his belt. "Share the peace," he told the boy.

"What you don't understand," he said, pointing a finger at Nieman, "is that the duplicity of the white man in Indian dealings has a long and bitter history. Probably began with the first 'Ugh' the white man heard from an Indian."

"Ugh?" Nieman was puzzled.

"Yes, just like in the old cowboy and Indian movies. The white man may have interpreted that 'Ugh' as a friendly 'hello,' but the Indian probably meant, 'You white guys are a pack of thieves. Get lost.'" He laughed.

Nieman didn't know whether to chuckle or take the remark seriously. He hadn't expected a joke, much less sarcasm.

The Native American smiled and said, "I'm just toying with you, Mr. Nieman. Even we Indians have a sense of humor. We just don't show it often. But we do laugh a lot—mostly about you white men. You know how many Indians it takes to screw in a light bulb?"

"No," said a perplexed Nieman.

"One fewer than the white man needs."

"Oh?"

"Oh, yes. We don't need a guy to read the instructions, but if we did need them, we'd have them sent by smoke signals."

Nieman at this point couldn't help but laugh out loud, as did several pedestrians who had stopped by to hear what had prompted their homeless "Indian Joe" to engage in such a long conversation. The lengthy dialogue by now had drawn a small crowd around Nieman and the Indian.

"We all live with preconceived notions of others."

Nieman nodded.

"Before your Civil War, Lincoln said slavery wasn't all that bad a thing and okay if it stayed in the South. But Robert E. Lee spoke out against slavery. Your great baseball hero, Ty Cobb, Hall of Famer, was thrown in jail a number of times for fistfights he got into, one time with an umpire and many times with his wife."

The crowd of onlookers grew, and some responded with shouts of "Right on" and "You tell him, Indian Joe." A few raised clenched fists. A flash shot through Nieman's mind that he might wind up in court, accused of inciting an urban riot in downtown Indianapolis.

The Indian looked Nieman straight in the eyes. "Everything depends on your viewpoint, my young friend. From a distance the mountain may look like a steep climb, but the approach to the summit can look steeper and even more intimidating to an exhausted climber."

Nieman stood transfixed. He didn't know how to respond.

"White Americans killed Indians before they knew them or understood them at all. Now they think Indians are just a bunch of dummies who can't hold their liquor. But the world—yours and mine—has changed," he said, leaning closer to Nieman.

"Today we Indians can claim doctors, military officers, lawyers, teachers, corporate CEOs, and even legislators—and I almost forgot, casino operators. We have many of those now. Talk about wampum." Some in the crowd laughed with him.

"The Indian is making a comeback, and always remember, the white man now is just another minority like us."

"Oh?" said Nieman, now flanked by the crowd of downtowners, all seemingly impressed with their homeless Indian's oratory.

"Your Census Bureau says so. Darker skins are coming on strong, cowboy, and we Native Americans have our own grievances, just like the others."

"I'm aware the American Indians were shortchanged and sold out many times in peace treaties and land contracts—," Nieman said.

"*Screwed* would be the proper word, Mr. Nieman."

Onlookers backed him with angry shouts. "He's right."

"The Indians were cheated."

"They have rights too."

One man kept shouting, "Peace, brothers."

Some fists were rising.

When the shouting and muttering died down, a nervous Nieman stroked his chin and then quietly asked the Indian, "Would you be willing to come down to Plainview for a visit, at my expense, just for a few days to revisit your old campgrounds?"

"You mean to see again my ancestors' land, where I was born and raised by the Shakers, where I fished and hunted, where my tribal spirits are still on the wind? It is for those who have disappeared that I beat my drum as well as for all Native Americans everywhere."

"Yes," said Nieman. "There are people there who remember the Indian encampment. I'm told you are the last member of the tribe?"

The Indian, suddenly pensive, looked off into the distance. "It's true. I am the last of the tribe. It would be rewarding to roam over the land again, while I still can. You know, Mr. Nieman, I am ninety-five years of age, so my memory is long." He paused. "I might consider your offer."

Nieman smiled and said, "You can stay at the hotel at no cost, and we have some food service too you can enjoy."

"Oh no, not necessary. And I'll pay for my own ticket, and I can live off the land. I won't accept any charity from the Silver Swan, which has left a footprint of dishonor in our tribal heritage."

"Oh? How so?" Nieman didn't expect an answer and didn't get one.

"A long story from many years ago. I prefer not to discuss this shameless matter of honor now. But yes, I will accept your offer, but not to discuss Indian real estate. I've learned not to trust white Americans in treaty arrangements, especially in dealing with Indian land."

"So be it," said Nieman. "I'll look forward to seeing you in Plainview. While you're there, I promise not to discuss real estate ... unless you call for a, ah, a pow wow." He chuckled at his own pun.

The Indian didn't, but with his arms folded over his chest, he responded with what Nieman thought was the hint of a smirk.

Nieman gestured a goodbye and shouldered his way through the gaggle of onlookers, who'd formed an agitated circle around the Indian. He worried some might be waiting for a protest march to start. Groping for a lemon drop in his pocket, he could only hope now that a visit by Indian Joe to his old homeland might give him another chance to talk real estate, despite what he'd promised.

Chapter 38

Waiting for Indian Joe

"Can you pick up our man at the bus station tomorrow? A social agency in Indy called to say he was coming, and I have a feeling he'd rather be greeted by you than me."

"Sure," said Missy. "But I'm taking Faith with me. She remembers the tribe a long time ago, so maybe she'll have more to talk to him about than I would. But where're we taking him?"

Missy and Nieman sat in her law office, watching her ink-jet printer spitting out copies of a business plan they hoped to present to the bank and investors, if his plan ever saw daylight.

"Just take him out to where he used to live with the tribe on the other side of the creek."

"Out by Faith's place." She paused as she took a stack of sheets from the printer. "You know, I've been thinking: If there's no tribe left, and he's really all alone, why wouldn't he want to sell the land? He's been homeless and accepting handouts on the street. You'd think he'd jump at an offer on the land—if it's his to sell."

"You'd think so. Maybe you could broach the subject. Without his release on that land, the bank won't give us a mortgage, even if we could come up with enough money."

"I'll try," said Missy, "but he'll probably think we're planning to build a theme park here or a casino and figures we have millions to spend. And he isn't even aware yet of what's below the ground. All that Civil War stuff and the wines are under the tribal strip of land."

"I know but—oh, I forgot to tell you something."

"Well?"

"My history professor at Emory called me back yesterday, and guess what?"

"What?"

"This is another you-won't believe-it thing. That letter we found from Grant to Lincoln? Well, one of the mysteries of the Civil War among historians is why Grant never responded to Lincoln's message congratulating him on the Vicksburg victory—and that could be the letter we found. Seriously."

"My God, that is amazing. It's got to be worth thousands."

"He said it's invaluable, and right away he insisted we give it to a museum like the Smithsonian. He really got worked up about it on the phone and asked to see it, so I sent him a photo of it."

"He's right of course," she said. "We'd have to share that one."

"I guess so, but you know, we could have a good copy of it made and then frame it and display it in the lobby after we get the place restored—if we can ever buy it."

"Incidentally, who are the people who might be in on this great venture, if we ever get it off the ground?" Missy asked.

"I have a couple of savings accounts, and then there's the mayor, and Faith wants in, and Curly has asked me about it too. But we're still way short on what's needed," Nieman said.

"Okay, and I'll be in too for a little. What's the bank need for the down payment, if we ever get that far?"

"About half of the sale price. They're asking $425,000, and my offer to the home office will be $390,000."

"So we'd have to come up with lots more money. Kind of frightening, isn't it?"

"The time to be scared is later because that's when any money will change hands—again, if we can ever come up with enough."

"And that's assuming we'll get a thumbs-up from our Indian friend, which doesn't look very likely, and from Madame Norton."

"A long shot to be sure. But right now I think we should just take a breather, unless you have clients coming in," Nieman said as he stepped in back of her and gripped her shoulders.

"I do," she said, "but if you massage my shoulders any longer, I'll cancel everybody."

"I'd love to, but I have to get back to the hotel. Boney and I are working on the rooms now. I told him I'd help again. Painting's getting to be my secondary specialty."

"What's your first?"

"Kissing beautiful women." Nieman leaned over and kissed her in the nape of her neck and then backed off. "Give me a call after you take our friend to the country. By the way, you have any dresses in your wardrobe with Indian designs? Flattery might give us an edge, even with an older Indian gentleman."

Chapter 39

Nostalgic Visit

When a stern Indian Joe stepped off the big Greyhound bus, Missy and Faith hurried to him through the small group of travelers getting off at Plainview. He said little in response to their cheery introductions but gazed intently toward the city's northern skyline, leaving both women wondering if he felt he'd made a mistake coming back to town.

They noticed that his tattered jeans, black porkpie hat with a feather, and the pigtail were as Nieman had described them. Both couldn't help but stare at the small drum the Indian carried, along with a small traveling bag and a pack roll slung over his shoulder.

"Ladies, forgive my pensiveness, but I am already feeling my ancestors here, so near to the home of their broken spirits." The chiseled copper face softened into an almost imperceptible smile as he settled into the rear seat of Missy's convertible and gazed at the passing scene. "It has been many years since I've felt this deep sensation. I hope you understand."

"Yes, we understand," Missy responded breezily as they turned onto the highway going to Faith's home. "By the way, if you don't mind, we're going to take you to Ms. Quinton's home, which, we think, is near your former tribal grounds. Is that okay with you?"

"Of course. That's the reason I've come here ... likely for the last time, I fear." He continued to gaze at the fields and patches of woods he played in as a young man, a landscape that likely hadn't changed much in the near half century since he last saw it.

"In fact ... ah, should we call you Mr. Eagleman, as I'm told is your Christianized name?" Faith asked with some hesitancy.

He nodded.

"Well, Mr. Eagleman, I have a small cabin in back of my home, and you're welcome to use that if you'd like while you're here with us."

"Not necessary, but I appreciate the offer. The good earth is enough for me. By day I only need a place in the sun, and at night only the moon to keep me company." He tapped his hand on the rolled-up pack over his shoulder and smiled.

"Of course ..." He paused. "If it rains, I might reconsider your offer. A roof does look better, I suppose, as we age, even to Indians."

Faith and Missy chuckled with him and glanced at each other with raised eyebrows, both thinking this guy was a genuine Indian, not just playing the role. And he had a good sense of humor.

"You know, Mr. Eagleman, when I was a little girl, we'd sometimes hike down to your encampment and ..."

Faith continued talking, and Missy was careful not to make any sudden stops or starts, relaxing her usually impatient foot on the accelerator pedal of her yellow Mustang

Eagleman put his head back and closed his eyes as Faith went on recounting the old days. Neither she nor Missy knew if he was sleeping or awake as they drove to Faith's home near that long-ago Indian campground, Mr. Eagleman's long pigtail trailing in the wind over the convertible's back seat.

Chapter 40

Note of Disappointment

Nieman pushed aside the hotel guest registers he'd been studying, leaned back in his office chair, and stared out the window. He'd had a feeling when he came to work that nothing would go right after Handley told him only five rooms were occupied overnight. The day only got worse when Missy called from Faith's house after a chat with Indian Joe.

"No, he didn't seem receptive to my suggestion of selling the tribal land," she said. "But I still think maybe there's hope. I'll tell you more when I get back."

But all Nieman could see was failure of Plan A, with no Plan B in hand. So he brooded, waiting for Missy to give him what he knew would be more bad news from her day in Indian country. He was finishing his third cup of coffee when she showed up.

"Please don't tell me if your news is all negative," said a depressed Nieman. "I already feel the bad vibes. I've been looking for a window in a tall building, but there isn't one in town." He forced a laugh and pressed his hands against his head like he had a bad migraine. "He's still talking no-go, right?"

"Well, not exactly but kind of. I still think he isn't greedy though. That's one good sign, so let's not get so downcast yet."

"I knew he'd be reluctant. I could tell it when I met him yesterday. He didn't shake my hand again."

"He's a complex guy, Lee. He told us that years ago he worked for a long time as a paralegal, which is why he's so articulate. Just don't be so negative."

"I'm just being honest with myself. We find all that exciting stuff, but we still don't have enough money, and we've still got an Indian with a grudge and that Norton woman with an attitude. So, we're still no closer to buying it. In short, I'm losing faith."

"I know. I know."

"And that's not all. My boss back in Atlanta called again to remind me I only have a couple of weeks to clear the deed and act on our sale agreement before they work out a deal with another buyer who wants to tear it down. And worse, the guys in Atlanta told me Sylvia's been calling the big boss and telling him the place should be torn down, which, of course, is just what he wants to do. The whole thing looks hopeless. I guess I knew it'd never work out."

"Aww, they have to honor your offer for a reasonable time. And any other buyer would face the same problem with the Indian and Sylvia. Listen, Lee, all kinds of people in losing situations didn't give up and eventually won. Did Lincoln give up when he got beaten in his first try to be a state legislator?"

"I don't know. I guess not."

"No. He didn't. And then look at George Washington after being trounced by the British in New York. In the middle of winter he only had a couple thousand men left, but did he quit? No, sir. He went on to beat them at Trenton.

"Did Paris give up because Helen of Troy was already married to another guy? Did the 101st Airborne give up at Bastogne? The Apollo 13 crew? The Browns—"

"The Browns?"

"The Cleveland Browns."

"Yeah," he said, "they don't give up, but they usually lose anyway."

"I know, but they always have good intentions. I'm just trying to make a point, Lee. Don't be so pessimistic. But I didn't drop by to give you a lesson in lost causes." She went on. "Actually, I think our Native American friend might just see things our way, if we're patient and maybe offer him something in return. Think about it: We'd be getting a piece of land, and he'd be getting nothing because I'm sure that he's definitely not interested in making money on the tribe's land."

"I thought you weren't going to bring up the subject of money with him."

"Well, I wasn't, but it kind of came up anyway, and I pressed him a little. Now I wouldn't bet on it, but I really think he might be persuaded to release the land if we could maybe structure a deal, maybe one that would benefit Native Americans in some way—or maybe build a monument honoring Indians."

"There's no tribe left," Nieman said.

"Not here, but he told me he chants and beats his little drum all day for Indians everywhere and for the spirits of his tribe's ancestors, even if there aren't any Chikopiks left here today."

"That's possible. By the way, did you ask him why he's the last Indian standing? Didn't he have any children?"

"Yes, I asked him, and no, he didn't have any children."

"Yeah, but what about the others in the tribe? They all couldn't have all been childless."

"This gets a little complex, but do you know anything about the Shakers?"

"No, I just remember reading that the last of the women all died off a few years ago."

"That's right—and for good reason. There was a Shaker colony here a long time ago, and the Indian tribe that was here was already shrinking and the federal government was encouraging the remaining young Indians to attend the Shaker schools in this area of Indiana. I guess they wanted to 'Christianize' them, Shaker style."

"So what? That couldn't be all bad."

"Depends on your viewpoint, Lee, but think about this: The reason there are no Shakers around today is the same reason there's only one Indian left here from the tribe."

"Huh?"

"The Shakers schooled the Indians well, mixing in a little religion. What the Shakers emphasized in their faith was abstinence, chastity. Sex was a no-no. The Indians were good learners and apparently took the schooling seriously. That's why there are no Shakers or Indians around here today—and why our friend is the last Indian standing from the tribe, long feather or no long feather."

"Wow. That's a quick answer to zero population growth. Hey, and no worries about affording college for the kids."

"No, but no fun either."

"That's all well and good, but it doesn't solve the problem. Maybe if we can figure out what the burr in his saddle is all about with the Swan, maybe we could remedy it and change his mind."

"I agree. Now he's going to stay around for a couple more days before going back to Indy. Maybe Faith can ask him exactly what the problem is. He's staying outside by her place."

"What do you mean, outside?"

"I mean he's camping out on the old Indian land across the creek from her house. I told him he could stay here at the Swan, but he turned that down flatly, like he did when you suggested it."

"Hmm. I guess we don't understand the Indian psyche," Nieman said.

"Guess not." Missy shrugged her shoulders.

"Well, I have some book work to do here. You mind calling Faith and ask her to maybe nail him down on his he hang-up on the Swan before he leaves?"

"Will do. Oh, by the way, he did tell me about that other name you mentioned he has, Long Feather. But I've got a couple of clients to see, so I'll tell you about it later. Bye."

She left, and Nieman grabbed the month's guest list he'd been looking at earlier, to see if guest revenue was trending up or down. Without looking, he feared the figures would further dampen his spirits.

CHAPTER 41

Drum Beat from the Past

The shelves behind his desk reached up to the high ceiling, each holding dusty cardboard boxes packed with inventories and records of the hotel's business from past years. Nieman had been on the job for only a month or so and hadn't thought about looking at them. Even the most motivated hotel manager wouldn't voluntarily decide to research his hotel's old business records without a compelling reason. Life is too short.

What the hell, he thought. His plan for the Swan was still in limbo, if not dead, and he had nothing important to do except to call a few local firms to pitch banquet business. He spun his swivel chair around, randomly grabbed one of the old record boxes, and plopped it down on his desk. Picking through the contents, he found occupancy tallies, expense records, and notes typed or handwritten by managers in the 1980s.

"Hmm," he said out loud. The guest figures showed an average of twenty-two guests a night in July of that year. "Almost full all month," a note in the margin read. Since he'd been there, the place had never been "almost full."

Turning a few more pages, he stopped when he found a penciled note with "John Glenn" in the day's register, with an attached handwritten note reading, "the astronaut running for office ... speech on balcony." The file held the signature he'd signed on that summer day in 1983, when he was making a bid for the Democratic presidential nomination.

Intrigued, Nieman began pulling other, earlier boxes off a shelf. A notebook in the 1950s box opened to the signature of Ernest Hemingway. A guest in 1954 had signed his name on a Swan dining room menu: "Stayed overnight ... said he liked our pheasant and oyster dressing," read a scribbled note stapled to the menu. Nieman read with some envy what the diners were offered that summer evening over forty years ago:

> Cucumber and sour cream mousse
> Tossed green salad
>
> Stuffed leeks
> Sauerkraut balls
> Stuffed mushrooms
> Oysters on the half-shell
>
> Pheasant with Smitane sauce, dressing
> Beef tenderloin, béarnaise sauce
> Chicken tetrazzini
>
> Baked squash
> Mashed potatoes in form
> Green beans, hollandaise
>
> Raisin-rhubarb pie
> Blueberry pie, apple pie
> German chocolate cake

Nieman reached up for earlier boxes. Leafing through papers from the 1880s, he found that most of the Swan's twenty-four rooms were at "full capacity" during each year's Christmas season. A scribbled note on a piece of paper remarked that the room rate had just been raised that week to $3.75 a night. A guest list from 1882 showed the name of Samuel Clemens, with a manager's note attached: "Filled the lobby with cigar smoke."

Anxious now to see what the very earliest year might reveal, he plucked some papers from the 1840s box and found notes about General William Henry Harrison: "Elderly general very friendly with staff. Gave brief talk after dinner." The register also showed the signature of Charles Dickens, who spent a night with his wife, who traveled with him "on a tour of the country." Nieman remembered hearing in his high school English class that Dickens wasn't pleased with what he found in America.

A doubled-over sheet of yellow paper caught his eye. He pulled it from the box. The notation was faded and almost illegible: "Indians left yesterday as danger passed. Had Mr. Hanson clean up cellar. Must get stored goods returned when possible." He read it again. He couldn't decipher the rest of the sentence, but that didn't matter. He was mesmerized momentarily.

"Oh boy!" he blurted out to no one. "Gotta be connected." He hurried to gather up all the papers and records he'd strewn around the floor and put them back in the appropriate boxes—all except one.

So worked up over what he'd found, he misdialed Missy's office number and had to dial it again. He stood by his desk, reading the words again in the long-ignored note in the Swan's log of activity.

"I'm telling you, Missy; this has to be connected with Indian Joe's grudge," he shouted on the phone.

"Could be, but calm down. I'm on speaker phone, and people in the outer office will hear you. What can you do about it?"

"Well, I'm not sure, but this is exciting, and it might explain his whole problem. Where's our Indian friend right now?"

"He's out by Faith's house, I think she's coming back to town with him later."

"How about asking her to tell him what I found and maybe she could get him to open up."

"I could go out and meet with both of them later today. This might be a good way to bring up the land thing again. I'll call you back tonight. Okay?"

"Okay, okay. Boy, this is getting to be like a Nancy Drew mystery, eh?"

"Yes, and if Faith and I can solve the mystery, you'll be the first to know."

CHAPTER 42

Sylvia's Penthouse Pitch

The Swinton Corporation's CEO, Stuart Tompkins, was not a self-made man. In fact, he was the grandson of one of the cofounders of the hotel chain. But everyone knew he had honestly worked his way up through the ranks—maybe not too energetically—of the hospitality giant, which operated properties in most major US cities. It was without much effort and certainly no sweat at all that he'd moved up the corporate ladder faster than his peers, but they liked him in spite of this. He was friendly and, above all, a low-handicap golfer eager to take on all comers, even duffers.

So, no one was especially surprised when the board chose Tompkins as top dog at forty-five. His family still held most of the shares, and he was the only one in the family who had shown any interest in the hotel business, while the rest just liked staying in Swinton hotels for free without lifting a finger.

Swinton executives didn't expect much change when Tompkins took the reins, and they didn't get much. A mild-mannered man, Tompkins was content to accept the status quo for the corporation, which was already experiencing stellar success with its long-range plan showing a steep growth trend and a rising share price long before he stepped into the penthouse office atop the Grande Arms in downtown Atlanta.

He had married a woman older than he, and by all accounts richer and more domineering. She ran his life at home and socially, sometimes even telling him how to run his business as well. His coterie of managers at work knew Tompkins was an "easy mark" for the women he dealt with, earning the nickname of "ol' round heels," as he easily rolled over on sales pitches, especially when the females were attractive and younger. He once contracted with a lady sales rep for laundry services for all the chain's properties and only later realized most already had in-house laundry operations.

Bob Prestik, Lee Nieman's old friend and boss and Swinton's operations chief, had had no problem talking the CEO into agreeing that the company should hold off razing the Swan property and honor their resigning employee's request to buy it. This was despite Tompkins' initial urge to simply clear the hotel site for a quick sale of the property. After all, the place had been a drain on the books ever since Swinton acquired it a few years ago. He was reminded of all that whenever Sylvia Norton called him. Tompkins had ignored the calls until his secretary told him she was a stockholder, though not a major one.

"Mr. Tompkins, ah, may I call you Stuart?" she said on her latest phone call.

"Of course, Miss Norton," he said, sitting back in his leather-covered cherrywood chair that matched his expansive desk. He had to listen, but he didn't really want to talk about a rundown property in Indiana. He sat back and looked out at the Atlanta skyline.

"Well, Stuart, there is talk in this town of saving and restoring the Silver Swan. I suppose you know my family founded the hotel over 150 years ago."

"Well, yes, of course I know." He didn't. No one had told him that, and normally he only dealt with 1-percent shareholders, which Sylvia wasn't.

She proceeded to tell him why she didn't want the hotel restored, how it was "tarnishing our family name," and "It can never really be restored to what it was in the glory days"—and so on. "Seeing it rot away makes me ill," said Norton.

"I appreciate your interest, Miss Norton, but we have a legitimate offer in our hands, and that makes it problematic. I do agree with you though. I want it torn down too."

"Yes. Restored it would still be a reminder of what used to be, and my family doesn't want that."

"Well, let me talk to my real estate department. Maybe we still have other options."

"Well, I hope so, for my family's sake. I'm so thankful for your appreciation of our position on this. I might say, Stuart, you sound like a well-educated man. May I ask, would you be a Princeton graduate?"

"Why, ah, no," he said, surprised by the question. "Ah, no. Penn State."

"Oh. You just sound so Ivy League."

"Thank you," he said. "I'm flattered … I guess." He pressed the disconnect and pushed his intercom button. "Miss Miller, would you call Bob Prestik and ask him to come by my office when he's free."

"You know, Bob," he told Prestik when he came to the penthouse, "I like that young man Nieman and hate to see him quit us. I like seeing ambition, but business is business. Tell him to get his deal over with or we send in the wreckers."

Prestik said he would push Nieman to move faster on closing, but he wouldn't push so hard that Nieman's plan would fail all together. After all, he was considering a stake in the venture himself, something he hadn't mentioned to the big boss.

"By the way, Bob," he said as Prestik got up to leave, "how old is this woman who called from Indiana?"

"Way older than you, Stuart. "

"Oh, I see."

"Why?"

"Just curious."

Chapter 43

Grudge Mist Clears

The phone call from Nieman's former boss about Sylvia Norton's pitch to Swinton's CEO was just one more headache for him as the fall afternoon wore on in southern Indiana. Just as Nieman switched off the office light to head to a local eatery, Missy called to tell him she and Faith had taken Indian Joe to the bus station for his trip back to Indianapolis.

"We got him on the bus, but more exciting is that we got him to talk a little. I'll be over in a few minutes."

"We had quite a day with our Indian friend," she said as she walked into Nieman's office. "Hey, let me sit in your chair. I want to know what it feels like to run a big hotel."

"Have at it," he said, rising. "I just hope you found out something about that old note I found."

"Well, kind of," she said, leaning back in the swivel chair.

"What'd you do, bribe him to talk?"

"Actually, I just bought him a Happy Meal, and he loved it. He's really a very nice man."

"A Happy Meal! You're kidding me?"

"No, that's what he said he wanted. Living off the streets, he said it doesn't take much to satisfy his appetite. Sure, we have a motive, but I was just showing him some old world hospitality."

"Hmm."

"He said his grandfather told him that, way before he was born—like over 100 years ago—the tribe needed to hide out when federal agents were combing the state for Indians—I guess, to do a census and maybe move them to a reservation up by the Great Lakes."

"Are we talking the Trail of Tears?"

"Oh, no, that was way earlier, and the Indians they marched to Oklahoma came from Georgia and North Carolina. Our man doesn't really know why the Feds were looking for Indians here. I'd guess the Indians just hid because they were afraid they might be forced to move out of the area."

She went on. "Anyway, Indian Joe's grandfather told him the local Indians hid from the feds for maybe a week in the Swan's cellar."

"Hmm."

"The way I understood him was that the Swan's owner then, or manager, was okay with that, but they had to put up something of value to make sure the hotel would be reimbursed somehow for any costs involved, like food and maybe damage they might cause."

"Like collateral?"

"I suppose. Anyway. the tribe had no money, but they had important tribal things like ceremonial chest plates and head dresses and sacred ornaments and talismans with spiritual symbols on them. The chiefs would only use these in ceremonies."

"Wow! That might explain the note I found in the office, but I still don't get what the problem is, or was."

"He wouldn't say exactly, but apparently later the Indians paid back the hotel for the food they'd eaten with semiprecious stones and maybe some silver. But I got the impression that maybe the hotel never returned the tribal stuff it was holding."

"Well, that beats all if it's true. You have to wonder why the owner back then wouldn't have returned their things. Maybe he scammed the Indians."

"Or maybe he died about the same time. I don't know."

"I don't know how all this is going to help us talk him into releasing the land. All that stuff would have long since disappeared, or somebody swiped it a long time ago," said Nieman.

"Could be so. I don't know how we'd ever make amends, much less talk him into letting the land go. Like I said before, he isn't interested in money, so a bribe wouldn't work."

"Guess not. Hey, maybe he has a weakness for women."

"Get serious, Lee. He's ninety-five years old. But it does look a bit hopeless, I'll say that."

There was silence. Nieman slumped in his swivel chair, stared at the wall in the dark, and figured the odds of working out a deal now with Mr. Eagleman were still long, about as good as his ex-wife relinquishing all future alimony payments. Looking for another job again looked like a better bet.

Missy broke the quiet in the room, when she suddenly noticed the penciled note Nieman had stuck on his desk drawer.

"Well, hello—what do we have here?"

Chapter 44

Opportunity in Translation

Missy snatched the note from the drawer and held it under the desk lamp to get a better view of the scribbled message.

"I guess it's just a reminder my predecessor left," said Nieman. "It was stuck to the back of that old chair over there in the corner."

"Looks like code."

"I don't know. Just toss it in the trash."

"Hey, I love word puzzles, and I can tell you right away I think it's a comparison of sorts."

"Really? How so?" He was suddenly interested again in the note.

"Well, if you were an attorney or a big sports fan, you couldn't miss the two letters in the middle: the *V* and the *S*. That's gotta be for *versus*. You know, Roe versus Wade, Yankees versus the Indians. Right?"

"I hadn't looked at it that way, but it could be."

"If I'm right, we have *c-h-a-n-t-v* matched against *s-f-i-n-v*. Now we just have to figure out what those letters mean."

"You know, I wonder if we're even reading the letters correctly. It's pretty sloppy handwriting," said Nieman.

"I don't know, but I think I know who'd recognize the handwriting of his former boss. Handley. Is he around?"

"He's home right now, but he's probably awake. I'll call him."

It wasn't long before Handley showed up to find his boss and Missy hunched over the office desk with a magnifying glass.

"Good afternoon, people. What's the mystery being solved?" Handley said.

"Thanks for coming in early, Charles. You mind taking a look at this note. I think it was written by your former boss. We'd like to interpret it."

Handley leaned over the desk and peered at the scribbling. "I believe, sir, he was reminding himself to check out something."

"How'd you know that?"

"The first two letters are his usual *c* and *k*. His lower case *k* looks like an *h* but you'll notice a slight crook in the second down stroke."

Missy and Nieman looked again. "I see what you mean," said Nieman. "So he wanted to check one thing against another and that leaves *a-n-t-v* versus *s-f-i-n-v*."

"Sir," Handley said, "if I might. I think the *ant* translates as *antique*. He used that abbreviation. As for the *v* I can only venture a meaning of *value*. Mr. Cole often talked of the value of the old furniture here. He watched endless broadcasts of *Antiques Roadshow* on the telly."

"I believe you've cracked the mystery, Charles," said an excited Nieman. "If we could only figure out the other side of the equation."

"The *S* is a capital letter, so maybe it means *Swinton*, but the *f* and *i-n* escape me," said Nieman. "The *i-n-v* looked to me like inventory at first, but the *f* ... wait a minute. The company keeps a furnishings category in its property inventory. Could be that maybe."

"But what was he referring to?" Missy asked.

"Maybe that old chair it was stuck to," said Nieman, gesturing toward the scooped-back wood chair he'd shoved back into a corner.

Missy rushed across the room to the chair. "I've looked at this before and wondered about its antique value."

"Sylvia called it a Klismos chair, or something like that, from the 1800s."

"Oh, boy, if that's what it is, it's worth lots," she said. "Over a thousand, I'd bet."

"For that rickety old thing?" Nieman was wide-eyed.

"Yes, but look at that beautifully carved wood—mahogany, I think. And after all, Lee, it was probably manufactured before the Civil War."

The three stared at the chair in silence.

Missy spoke first. "Why don't we take a look at the furnishings inventory and see what the company valued it at."

"It's here somewhere," said Nieman, scanning the shelves near his desk. "I've never looked at it before." He pulled out a thick ledger labeled "Furnishings" and started leafing through the pages.

"Here it is, I think: 'Wood-back (mahogany) chair with fiber seat, old, acquired pre-Swinton.' In 1989 they listed this one and one other like it upstairs in storage at seventy-five dollars each."

"Is there an inventory number shown for it?" Missy asked.

"Yes. 89-298."

Missy turned the chair over. "That's it."

"In other words," said Nieman, "he could have sold that chair at an antiques auction and made over $1,000. Charles, did you ever know him to sell off any antiques?"

"I don't believe so, but, ah, there was an instance in the month he left when I happened to see him and a local handyman carry off a couch in the lobby. When I looked the next day or so, there was another couch there as a replacement. The replacement is a very nice couch but not old."

"I noticed that old couch was gone too," said Missy. "Had the ball and claw feet. It sure looked Chippendale."

"Wow. I think he was on to something," said Nieman. "Could that be why the place finally turned a profit in his last month on the job?"

"Sir, he mentioned the possibilities to me often. He said many of the fine antiques are listed in the Swinton inventory as just ordinary furnishings. Some of the Wedgwood sets are listed as just ordinary chinaware, Chippendale pieces as just ordinary furniture, Shaker chairs as simply old chairs, and so on. He said the company had no idea of the values here in the antiques or the art. Mr. Cole referred to this as the Swan's 'hidden values.'"

Nieman turned to Missy. "Would that be legal? It's like the money is only going from one company pocket to another."

"I guess ... if the company knew what you were doing."

After she left, Nieman's thoughts turned to all the possible "hidden values" in the old ballroom chock-a-block with vintage discards. His predecessor may have inadvertently shown him a door he didn't know could be opened to help him buy the Swan, or at least pay the bills for a while.

Chapter 45

Something up Her Sleeve?

Nieman decided the next morning to put his hotel restoration plan worries out of mind by getting his hands dirty in a no-worry pursuit: painting. He threw on an old pair of jeans, a well-worn tee shirt and a ball, and dropped a couple of slices of bread in the toaster.

Back in the hotel, he said his usual "good morning" to Handley and the few housemaids who were there and headed for the utility closet, where paint was stored.

He headed upstairs to finish work he and Boney had started on the Harriet Beecher Stowe Room and instantly wished he'd asked Boney to join him today. The four-poster bed was too heavy for him to move away from the wall by himself. That wall would have to wait for now.

He turned to the adjoining wall and filled the paint tray with an azure blue. Ms. Stowe might have appreciated it but would likely have preferred the busier Victorian design of the original wallpaper now sunk under decades of paint layers.

A few minutes into paint-rolling, his phone buzzed from the front desk. He held off responding, finished the wall, and then headed downstairs, where he was told Faith Quinton had called. He phoned her.

"Faith? This is Lee at the hotel. What can I do for you?"

"Well, I've been thinking about your problem with Sylvia Norton, and I believe I might be able to help with that, maybe. It's been in front of me all this time, but I just didn't see it. You follow me?"

"Ah, not exactly, but I'm certainly listening." He'd almost forgotten about Sylvia while agonizing on the deal-breaker deed problem with Indian Joe.

"I guess what I need to ask is if you mind if I talk to her about possibly relenting on her interest in the Swan if it's sold. You know I have my own interest in this now, since I'll have a stake in your plan too—a small one, of course."

"Yes, I know, and I appreciate your concern and investment dollars. No, I certainly don't mind if you get involved. I assume you would be, ah, careful about what you say to her? We don't want to further ruffle her feathers."

"Oh, rest assured. I'll present my idea to her with extreme care. We go way back, and I know exactly how to deal with her."

"I'm sure you do, Faith, and I'll be pulling for you, whatever you're up to. Now, you are aware that she doesn't want the hotel restored either, mainly because she thinks it would be just a cheap replica of what it used to be Might I ask what you have in mind?"

"I just can't tell you right now, but I will if I have any luck. Let's say we'll be talking about a family secret—but not my family, mind you," she said.

"Okay, Faith. Naturally I hope you succeed with whatever you are going to do. Just keep me posted."

"Oh, I will. I will. Thanks so much, and bye now."

Nieman hoped she didn't have murder in mind. He might be seen as an accomplice and even Attorney Landrew might have trouble handling that kind of case.

Later, when he'd made his way back to his apartment to watch a Colts game, he knew sleep wouldn't come easily. As he watched the Eagles beating the Bears, all he could think about was the skirmish Faith would be getting herself into with Sylvia. He just hoped it wouldn't drive Sylvia to visit him again.

Eventually he rose from the couch and headed to his bed, with visions of Indian Joe in his porkpie hat, the long feather still dangling from the brim. Maybe the whole idea of buying the Swan wasn't worth all these worries. Maybe looking for another career was still a better option.

CHAPTER 46

Indian Joe Nostalgic

Most riders had no problem catching some sleep in the cushiony seats of the Greyhound bus taking Indian Joe back to Indianapolis. But for him it was almost too soft compared with the hard ground he usually slept on under an interstate overpass near Indy's downtown. And his fellow travelers were quieter than his usual companions, half of whom by nightfall were typically boisterous and drinking away the day's booty from generous Hoosier downtowners. For this Native American, daydreaming seemed the better escape as the bus roared northward and dusk closed in on the passing landscape.

He stared out the wide window by his seat, watching the dimly visible harvested fields and patches of dark forests go by. He thought about the years he'd spent here with his young Indian pals, playing in those same woods and fields. The sights of his tribal land after all those years away had sent him on a journey of memories.

He remembered as a boy searching for blackberries and raspberries in the hot summers, papaws as they ripened, and nuts from the trees and playing war games with other tribal youngsters. They'd make their own bows and arrows with blunted points for mock battles. Some of the older boys would use tactics they'd heard their fathers and grandfathers talk about in skirmishes with other tribes in the misty past and with settlers who came to take their land.

He remembered many nights sitting by open fires by the creek they called Crawfish Creek. Everyone would listen as passed-down stories of the tribe's past glories were told—and likely embellished by the latest teller he realized as he aged.

At tribal council meetings he and other youngsters—his group called themselves the "young warriors"—would sit behind the chief and the elders and just listen. He recalled one elder who would always offer advice to the young people on the best way to hunt deer and trap beavers but also on how to lead a worthy life. He recalled the elder's words: "The spirit of the forest provides the way of many trails, but it is up to you, young warriors, to choose the correct trail to reach your goal."

Another elder would always respond with, "When that mother bear chased you long ago, did it matter which trail you took to run on instead of standing still?" And everyone would laugh because they knew that the elder telling the story was once clawed by a bear in the forest when he got between a mother bear and her cubs.

Indian Joe liked best to hear war stories his father and uncles would tell about their fathers and grandfathers fighting many years ago in real wars, like the Battle of Tippecanoe up north by the Wabash River. Later in school he learned that the Shawnee chief Tecumseh tried to get all the tribes like the Chikopiks into an alliance, but not all the tribes joined in, and they were beaten by William Henry Harrison when he was a general in the army. But now there were no bears to hunt and no battles to fight in, and that proved to be a lifetime worry for Indian Joe because his became a generation of warriors without a cause.

The bus made a brief stop at Bloomington, and most of the passengers got off to buy sandwiches and soft drinks. Indian Joe stayed seated, reached into his backpack, and pulled out a package of peanut butter crackers. That took him back to the old days at the campgrounds, when everyone in the tribe would share food, whether it be berries or a fresh kill of a deer, rabbit, or squirrel.

That brought something else into soft focus in his mind as the passengers reboarded and the bus merged back on the interstate highway. As he nodded off, he thought again about Missy Landrew's question about the origin of his Indian name. He couldn't remember how old he was when he found that injured eagle, but he remembered nursing its broken leg and then releasing it.

He remembered too the pride he felt in being recognized with the Long Feather name, but as he grew older, he wasn't bothered when, after moving to Indianapolis, nontribal people began calling him Indian Joe. He knew the downtown strangers liked him and liked the sound of his drum echoing around the tall buildings, though many were unaware of why he chanted and why he beat the drum. He told those who asked that he was praying to the spirits for all Indians, for their sorrows in suffering past betrayals.

He explained his Indian name to Missy because he'd come to respect her and feel comfortable around her. And, he admitted to himself, he liked the Swan's new manager as well, finding him not quite the heartless white businessman he'd expected. After all, the man knew the Swan's dishonor of the tribe went back over a century ago.

But Indian Joe did regret telling the Swan's manager he was the last living member of his tribe. He wasn't certain of that, but all the others had moved away or died. He alone felt the responsibility of standing tall for the tribe, even as it vanished. He knew from his work as a paralegal he could legitimately sign documents as the tribe's only known remaining representative. Only he who was left could speak for those who were gone. Only he, who had finished high school and gone on to work in the legal field, could knowledgeably sign any quit claim on the land the Swan's would-be owner wanted.

Indian Joe didn't want to give up the tribal rights to the land. *But*, he thought, *what will happen to the land when I'm no longer around? In the end, will anyone ever remember how sacred the land once was, or that the Chikopik tribe once called it home?*

As the Greyhound continued on its way north, he nodded off, thinking about that and his lost tribe and wondering where all the young warriors were now, if not dead.

CHAPTER 47

Light Bulb in a Dream

Nieman sat upright in his bed, still caught up in a nightmarish dream: a misty vision of long, white feathers falling off a wide-brimmed Stetson, the feathers distorted, twisting and turning as they floated to the ground. He pinched his eyes and glanced at the clock: 4:30 a.m. Except for a small nightlight, the apartment room in the carriage house was dark and very quiet, until he shouted, "Feathers? Feathers! That's gotta be it."

He shook his head to make sure he wasn't still sleeping and tried hard to recapture the dream that had ended so abruptly with feathers fluttering down around him and the cowboy hat warped and stretched out of shape. He slammed his fist into his palm. He knew what he had to do.

In a Eureka moment, Nieman leaped out of bed like a man possessed, threw on the battered pair of jeans lying in a bundle on the floor, where he'd left them after the painting job, and tied on a pair of sneakers. He forced himself to calm down but still felt foolish, glad no one was around to see him rushing around like a mad man. *It was all probably a big mistake anyway*, he thought as he grabbed a flashlight from a bureau drawer.

He had to take another look at that dirty canvas bag he'd seen underground. He had to know. Could it still be holding an Indian tribe's treasure? He convinced himself it was as he raced for the back door of the Swan. Maybe his imagination was playing tricks on him. Maybe what he really saw in that dreadful bag was what he first thought it was: discarded rubbish with a bad odor.

Suddenly he felt ridiculous, on a wild goose chase just to satisfy a lust to unravel a puzzle he'd constructed from no more than thin air and a few faded memories of an old Indian.

Handley would be somewhere in the hotel, but Nieman hoped he'd be back in the bar, matching the cash register tape against the cash drawer. He tiptoed through the lobby, making as little noise as possible, heading for the cellar door. He didn't want anyone to catch him on a venture that could be seen as crazy if not downright pointless in the end.

He'd made repeated trips into the far end of the tunnel and had brought everything of value upstairs—everything but the canvas bag. Bent down and breathing hard, he groped through the tunnel, reassuring himself that even if he were wrong about the bag, he was certain he'd never make another trip into this dark unpleasant place. Finally, coming into the open area at the end of the tunnel, where he'd discovered the Civil War relics and the bag, he flashed the beam of light around.

There it was, just as he had left it, crumpled in a corner, still covered with mold and partly rotted. He tugged at the opening and instantly was reminded of the putrid, disgusting odor that had repulsed him when he first opened it. Holding his breath and aiming the flashlight down into the opening, he looked deep into the bag.

"I'll be damned," he said into the darkness. He didn't remember seeing so many feathers the last time, but as he tried to pull some out to take a closer look, he couldn't. They were all held together by a beaded leather strap that had become stiff and cracked with age.

"This is no bird," he said out loud, his voice muffled in the darkness. He tried to take a deeper look but couldn't see what lay beneath the feathered strap, and the smell was too pungent. He let the feathers and strap drop back into the bag.

"Phew! Lemme outta here," he said to no one. It didn't matter what else was in the bag. He knew he'd found the headdress left there well over a century ago.

As he struggled to pull the bag across the tunnel's rough floor, he didn't need a scale to tell him the bag held more than just a pile of feathers. He spent the next half hour on all fours, lugging it behind him to the hotel cellar. At the top of the stairs he flung open the door and shouted, hoping his night auditor would be close by now, and sober.

"Handley, a little help here, please."

Handley came, wide-eyed. "Good grief, sir. I see you've been exploring again. More wines? How can I help?"

"No wines this time, my man," he said as he backed down the steps, with Handley following. "There's a heavy load down here you can help me with."

As they muscled it up the steps to the lobby, all Nieman could think was that this package may be disgusting, but it might just hold the key to patching up an ancient feud over a matter of "dishonor."

Chapter 48

Misty Past in a Poke

After dragging the bag to a back room on a house service dolly, the two men began emptying it, Nieman explaining to Handley what it could mean to his plan for the hotel. Carefully, they pulled out the feathered strap. Indeed it was the headdress Nieman had expected to see. But the woven and beaded leather strap that held all the gray and white feathers had hardened over the years and was moldy and partly disintegrated. Only the colorful beading between the quill shafts seemed intact. Nieman held it up, but some pieces of the band separated and dropped to the floor. "Boy, wouldn't this look great if we could get it restored?"

"Yes, sir, it must have been a handsome outfit," said Handley as they pulled out a tangle of other leather strappings.

To Nieman these looked like leg wrappings and armlets, both with feathers attached and embossed with curious symbols. One wide piece of tooled leather caught his interest. He guessed it might have once served as a ceremonial chest plate. Small pearls and beading lined the edge. He remembered reading somewhere that freshwater pearls could come from river oysters.

"Do you think this is actually the lost collateral, as you called it, sir?" Nieman had recounted for Handley the tale of the Indians hiding at the Swan.

"I wish I knew, but what else could it be? This whole venture has been unimaginable and puzzling, Curly—but fascinating too."

"Indeed. I suppose so." Handley was coaxing what appeared to be a partly disintegrated woven mat out of the bag, along with two what they guessed were beaver pelts. Designs were painted on the bare side and semiprecious stones lined the pelts at the edge. Judging from the yellowish color, they appeared to be amber.

"No wonder this bag was so heavy." Nieman was pulling out numerous ornamental silver pieces, flat silver dollar–size disks engraved with symbols, along with an assortment of flint arrowheads and other stones, some polished. He looked closely at one greenish stone and remembered a stone like it in a rock collection he had as a youngster.

Handley held up his next find. "A tomahawk, perhaps?" The wood shank was carved with what they guessed were spiritual Indian emblems. Leather strips held a sharpened flint stone, and feathers hung from the butt end.

They pulled out several leather necklaces, some strung with raptor talons and beading, others with beads and pearls. Another thong was festooned with what looked like animal fangs.

The two spent another half hour emptying the bag and spreading everything on the floor, including several elk-like statuettes carved in wood. They sat on the floor for a few minutes, gazing in silence at what the bag had held.

"You know, Charles, you can't help but have deep feelings when you see all this stuff, like beads that some primitive tribe treasured. Today it'd be silver dollars or bank savings accounts. Makes you wonder about what's important in life."

"Without a doubt, sir."

"Let's just get this headdress to a taxidermist. Maybe he'll know how to bring it back to life. It'll need a lot of help."

"I'd suggest, sir, the first thing we do is get rid of this," said Handley, pointing to the empty bag. "It has to have the most objectionable stench I've experienced since being stuck for a few days in a foxhole in Normandy."

"I know, Charles, but that odor might be the sweet smell of a peace treaty with an old Indian. I've got to take some pictures of these things and send them off to our man in Indy. Maybe this would convince him to come back and see it all in person."

Nieman got up from the floor. "I've got some calls to make."

The first was to a sleepy Missy. "You're really not going to believe this one. I had this dream about feathers flying around everywhere and …"

Chapter 49

We Talking Blackmail?

Later in the day Missy came to the hotel and quickly vetoed the taxidermist idea after she saw what he'd found. She had a friend who was a curator at the Louisville Natural History Museum. "They do this sort of thing all the time. I'll call him."

"Yes, but let's get hold of Indian Joe right away too. Face it—he's the only one who can tell us if this is the real McCoy, so to speak."

"But how would he really know? This all happened way before he was born."

"He'll know. He's heard all the stories about it. I mean what else could it be? And maybe, just maybe, giving it all back to him will bring him around on the property."

"A sentimental bribe?" she asked.

"Something like that. It's worth a try, if we can get in touch with our friend again and send him pictures of all this."

A knock came at the storeroom door. "What's up?" he asked the clerk who'd knocked.

"A Mrs. Quinton is here to see you. She said it's kind of important."

"Great. Just ask her to go to my office. I'll be there in a couple of minutes." Missy joined him as he greeted Faith.

"Oh, Mr. Nieman and Miss Landrew, so glad to see you both," said a breathless Faith Quinton with an ever-so-slight smile. "I hope I haven't interrupted anything important, but I'm so excited about this, and I know you'll want to hear what I've been up to."

"Of course, we would," he said, pulling his chair closer to the couch where Faith and Missy sat, his mind reverting to the problem of Sylvia Norton.

"Well, I thought about her objection to your plan, and then it struck me. I had the answer all along right in front of me. And now I think her meddling is, as they say, water over the dam."

Nieman and Missy glanced at each other, eyebrows raised, both on the edge of their seats. "We're all ears, Faith."

"Now there is a caution here," said Faith, with Missy and Nieman at the edge of their seats, waiting for her to reveal her scheme. "You'll both have to keep this to yourselves. I'm pledged to secrecy as part of the bargain with Sylvia. But I'm getting ahead of myself."

She reminded them of the rumors of a ghost haunting the Swan and that "people who've seen it always see it in the Grant Room. My grandfather saw the ghost too, one time. He managed the Swan then and was close to one of the Norton sons, who told him when he was on his death bed the secret behind the ghost story."

"The ghost," Faith went on, "was—or is, legend says — a girl in her late teens, who General Grant secretly visited from time to time when he came to town during the war."

"Aha," Nieman said. "The paramour, the warrior back from the front line for some R and R."

"Well, of course, the man did work hard winning all those battles," Faith said. "But in any case, she became pregnant by him and died in childbirth. The poor child, a girl, was taken in by the Norton family. They raised her as their own because the general never claimed the child as his. He was away a lot, of course, at the war and all. Anyway, that illegitimate child turned out to be Sylvia Norton's grandmother. Isn't that a stitch? Talk about your proper family tree."

"Boy, that is a shocker," said Nieman. "But what's that have to do with her agreeing to give up her stake in the Swan?"

"Well, her decision wasn't exactly voluntary. Remember, I told you I was writing a book on the town's history and the hotel's history. So, with Sylvia I merely implied that I might be able to avoid mentioning her family secret as part of our town's history if she would agree not to hinder your plan to restore the Swan."

Nieman and Missy, eyebrows raised, looked at each other.

"She was shocked, of course. I've never seen such a look, but I loved it. You know, when I was a little girl and she was a teenager, and we'd both be at the hotel sometimes, and she'd snub me and tell me I shouldn't mingle with the guests, even if my father was manager. This is what I call getting even."

"In a word, you blackmailed her," said a grinning Nieman.

"Well, I merely suggested the possibility of going public with her real heritage, an illegitimate grandmother. Serves her right. Besides, I want to see the place restored. It'll bring back so many memories for me, and for a lot of other people in town. Oh, it's so exciting. I don't think I've been aroused about anything since my honeymoon with my first husband ... or was that the third?"

"Faith," he said, laughing and reaching for her hand, "Missy and I think you've done a wonderful thing, and we'll keep the secret between us. It's certainly a load off my shoulders. And that leaves only one more problem to figure out, and we'll be home free—well, not exactly free, I guess." They all laughed.

"Oh, but, Mr. Nieman, I didn't tell you the other part of my agreement—and I do hope I didn't assume too much."

"I'm sure you used good judgment, Faith," said Missy. "Go on."

"Well, in exchange for her backing off, she wants the ballroom on the fourth floor—after you've restored it—named after her family. Her words were 'the Norton Grand Ballroom,' to be exact … and …"

"And what?"

"She wants a bronze plaque mounted in the ballroom, recounting the Swan's history and its founding by—of course—her great-grandfather."

Nieman and Missy looked at each other, raised their fists in the air, and shouted "Yes" in unison. "We'll do it. By God, life is good," said Nieman.

"But you know, Lee," said Missy, "our Indian might turn out to be more stubborn than Sylvia."

"Yeah, maybe, but right now let's drink to one success. How about it, Faith? Our bar is packing wine now. How about some Chardonnay?"

"Well, it's a little early for me, but I think I might. This has been some experience. I just hope she, ah, passes away before I do."

"Why?"

"I told her I'd keep her secret, but what I didn't tell her was that when she passes, I'll feel free to revise my history of the town and reveal her real lineage in that revision. I mean keeping this secret is killing me."

They all enjoyed a few minutes of mirth over that as Nieman and Missy took Faith's arms in theirs and headed to the Swan's freshly painted barroom.

Without Faith noticing, the two winked at each other, happy to have been broadsided by the juiciest scandal in the town's history, even though it was a juicy scandal they couldn't share with anyone else.

Chapter 50

Long Feather Meditates

The distance from Indianapolis to Plainview was only about a hundred miles or so, but to Nieman it seemed like a thousand miles because of his passenger's silence.

"He hardly said a word during the whole trip," he told Missy as the two sat in the Swan lobby a few days after Faith's revelation. "I was beginning to wish I hadn't gone up there, but I didn't know how else to show him photos of the stuff I'd found."

"Did that get his attention?"

"For sure, and he did talk a little when he saw the pictures. He just didn't say much on the trip back here, except that he had 'much to think about' now. He said he'd have to meditate."

"Meditate?"

"He said he had to meditate with 'the spirits on the wind' when I first showed him the photos of the relics in downtown Indy. He just sat down on the curb and stared at each picture. After a while he told me all he wanted to do was ponder his life's mission and why he alone was left to carry on the tribal legacy.

"He said more than once he had to meditate on it, and right now that's what he's doing out in the country across the creek from Faith's house. I told him you or Faith would check on him in a few days and bring him here to show him the actual relics once all the restoration work is finished."

"So, you didn't bring up the subject of the Indian land and what we're trying to do?"

"No. He was too quiet. It was kind of uncomfortable to tell the truth. I think he knows what we want. I just hope he's thinking about deciding. Frankly, I can't get it out of my mind with a deadline coming up fast."

"I know, Lee, but remember this man has heard all about this stuff for years, and this is probably the biggest thing that's ever happened to him, so that's what he's likely reflecting on, not your plan for the hotel."

"I know. I'm just so worried. I can solve the money problem by releasing some of that 'hidden value' in the ballroom, and Faith has taken care of Sylvia. But he holds the final key now to the whole plan, and the CEO's deadline is closing in."

"Maybe I can help there."

"Like how?"

"You told me the Swinton CEO is pliable. Isn't that the word you used?"

"Yes, so?"

"So, maybe I could fly to Atlanta next week and do a little persuading."

"Yeah, I guess that might work. You'd do that for me?"

"No. For us."

"I think I love you," Nieman said.

"You better, mister," she said as she rose to leave. She winked and blew him a kiss. "You're going to pay for that trip to the Peach State. But l love you too. Bye now."

With Missy on her way to Atlanta, a bored and depressed Nieman found himself driving out of town. By now, everyone in Plainview knew an elderly Indian was camped out in the countryside and the Swan's manager wasn't the only local who'd driven out to see him in the field along the highway that passed the Quinton rock home.

But he was the only spectator who worried about how long the Indian would meditate. Pessimistic, he still figured the odds on the Indian releasing the tribal land at the Swan were about as good as his ex-wife relinquishing her rights to future alimony payments, regardless of what happened at Swinton's headquarters.

An extended deadline might prove useless anyway, he realized. Long Feather had already spent days meditating on the ancient Indian grounds and showed no sign of wrapping up his solitary séance.

He pulled to the berm and looked across Chikopik Creek to see Indian Joe squatting on the ground by the lean-to tent he'd brought from Indianapolis. The moment Nieman shut off the ignition, he could hear the drum beat, and when he listened very carefully, he could hear chanting as well.

Nieman still hoped Missy could sway Swinton's CEO to give him a few more agonizing days to wait out Indian Joe's meditations with the "spirits on the wind" before the wrecking ball was booked for the Swan. Just maybe the restored tribal relics would turn the trick. He could only hope … and wait.

Chapter 51

A Play for Time

Plainview's female attorney wasn't having a happy moment. She found herself cooling her stiletto heels far too long in the outer office of Swinton's penthouse executive office. Wearing her best knit dress with hemline too far above the knee, she planned her pitch for more time and waited to meet Stuart Tompkins.

But Swinton's chief was busy with his new office toy, an indoor putting green.

Missy was forced to sit idle for a half hour, while he tried out his new putter, knocking a few golf balls around on the floor to a cup that flipped balls back to him. Finally, glancing at his CCTV monitor of the waiting area, he spotted her. He dropped his putter quickly, opened his inner office door, and introduced himself, stunning his secretary who'd seldom seen him greet a visitor in the outer office.

"My dear, I'm so very sorry about keeping you waiting." All smiles, he took her hand in his and escorted her to the couch in his office. "I had some overseas business to attend to. Why don't we just go to lunch now to discuss your, ah, situation? You'll love the menu at the Atlanta Club. I'm a member there, and it's quiet, so we can talk. I'll call for a driver."

"You know, Mr. Tompkins," she said as they sat back in the company limo's leather seats, "I'm always so impressed with how top management of such a giant company is able to keep a finger on all the operations." She'd learned long ago that flattery was the best stimulant for conversation.

"Please call me Stuart, dear girl—no formalities here. The answer is to have a great staff. They do most of the thinking day in and day out, you know. I'm just the centerboard in the sailboat, making sure we stay on a straight course to our goal."

"Well, of course," she said, "and a straight course it has been. I've noticed your dividend always seems to grow." She'd done her homework for stroking his ego.

"Well, we do try to reward our investors," he said as the limo pulled up to downtown Atlanta's most exclusive club.

Seated in the wood-paneled dining room, Missy cut to the chase. Without mentioning the Indian's role, she said Swinton's new Swan manager might have a "slight problem" in clearing the land title quickly and hoped he'd understand. "I know you're a very busy man with huge responsibilities, but we thought you might ease off a bit on the deadline before tearing it down or selling it to someone else."

"Oh, my dear young lady, let's not worry about that," he said as the club waiter at the table asked, "Your regular wine selection, sir?" Tompkins nodded and turned to Missy. "Chardonnay all right with you? French, of course. It's a chateau I buy several cases from each season." She smiled and put on her impressed look.

They talked about her legal work and about the Swan's potential as a restored period hotel.

"You know, we hate to lose Lee. He's such a good man, but he did get us into a kind of messy public relations tangle here. But we knew he'd succeed whatever he got into, and we certainly don't want to stand in the way of ambition."

"I'm so pleased to hear you say that, Stuart. I do think his idea for the Swan will work out, assuming you'll give us a few more days to get our ducks in line, so to speak."

"Consider it done, my dear, but let's order now." He gestured at the waiter and turned to her. "I recommend the Monte Cristo sandwich."

"Thank you, but a green salad will do. Must watch the calories, you know," she said.

"Of course, my dear," said Tompkins, winking at her. "You know best."

As they ate, Missy realized she didn't need to unveil the bargaining chips she'd dreamed up on the flight to Atlanta. There was no need to tell him the Swan's menus could carry the Swinton logo or that both Swinton and the Swan could make joint use of a tall interstate sign or that Swinton employees could enjoy free lodging at the Swan. It was obvious he was already sold.

To ensure she'd heard him correctly, she said, "So, a few more days would be okay? Small as we are, we are prepared to make some concessions for your patience, like carrying the Swinton logo on our menus and—"

"Oh, my dear, I'm sure you and Mr. Nieman have done some creative thinking over this, but you needn't have bothered. I think we have an understanding. Tell Lee we'll give him another week to get the deed cleared. Okay?"

"Oh, yes, Stuart. That would be perfect. Thank you so much."

"Well, then, let's just wish you success with your plan."

He reached for the bottle on the table and filled both their stemmed glasses. "Here's to success at the Swan." They toasted with a clink.

He looked at her intently for a moment and pulled his chair closer to her at the table's corner. "I've been thinking, young lady, I'm very impressed with the way you handle yourself—businesswise, of course. By coincidence, we have an opening in our legal team for a regional attorney based in Indianapolis. You could represent us on legal matters there and in Chicago and Fort Wayne. Would you be interested?"

"Well, ah, frankly, I'm not sure what to say." Caught off guard, she kept hedging on an answer as they walked to the limo, which had pulled up at the front door.

"Now, of course, you wouldn't have to quit your practice in Indiana," he said as he opened the limo door for her.

"My man here will take you to the airport. I have another car waiting for me. I have some business downtown. But I do hope you'll take my offer seriously." He took her hand. "I certainly think you'd enjoy working on our team, and of course, you'd have instant authority from my office if you'd ever need that."

"I'll certainly keep it in mind, Stuart. It's been so nice talking with you. Bye for now."

She kept smiling at him as she climbed into the limo, wondering how she'd ever turn him down without turning the Swan's restoration plan on its head.

Chapter 52

Bribe in a Box?

It was a bumpy flight back from Atlanta, but Missy got a more pleasurable jolt when she called her office from the baggage area of Indy's International Airport.

"Fed-Ex just delivered this huge package a few minutes ago," her excited secretary told her.

"Who sent it?"

"Hold on a minute. Oh, here it is. It was shipped by a museum in Louisville."

"We know what that is for sure," said Missy. Her next call was to Nieman. "Can you take it to Faith's, so she can give it to our meditating Indian? This might spark him into a decision, you know."

"I do know, but I kind of feel guilty, like we're trying to bribe him. I've got my fingers crossed, though. But how'd the meeting go in Atlanta?"

"He's a sweet man, Lee. I have good news, and part of it will really surprise you. And he will give us a little more time. But I'll tell you all about it when I get back. Just get the package out to our friend. Let's get this over with. I'm tired of all this running around. I do have clients to see, you know."

"I know, but just remember, I love you."

She giggled as she glanced at the luggage conveyor belt. "Gotta go. My bag's here. I'll be back pretty soon. Bye. Love you too."

"Hello, everyone," Missy shouted with a big grin as she raced into the Swan lobby and spotted Nieman talking to Handley before he headed home. "Boy, do I have something to tell you."

"Great," he said, embracing her and kissing her on the cheek. "I think I may have some good news too, after seeing what was in that box."

"How'd it all look?"

"I didn't take everything out, but the headdress looked great, just like in the old movies, except we don't have an Indian chief on a horse wearing it. Faith just called and said he's looking at it all right now. I'm just hopeful."

"I'm hopeful too, Lee, and I missed you." They kissed again, and Handley cleared his throat audibly and headed for the front door. "Ahem … another day, another shilling, I suppose. Cheers."

They both chuckled, and Missy turned to Nieman. "You know, you might think twice about quitting your company so soon."

"Huh? I'll rethink it if our Indian doesn't give us an okay."

"I know that, but what I meant was if you do quit, you might miss out on working directly with executive management—on a very familiar basis." She smiled and then told him about the job offer and her conviction that the Swinton CEO "must have been a real ladies' man when he was younger."

Nieman chuckled. "Hey, I'm told he still is, but tell me more about that job offer. After all, I think I have a vested interest to protect."

"Oh, don't worry." She took his hand. "He's too old for me. But you haven't asked me about the most important reason I went there in the first place."

"Well?"

"We get another week at least."

"That's great, but maybe we won't need it. You know, it wasn't a half hour after I took the box out to Faith's that she called. She said Indian Joe was really anxious to see what the restored stuff looked like, and she's pretty sure that might be what will win him over."

"Sure hope so."

"Maybe we'll get lucky. You know, just for fun, when I was coming to the office this morning, I threw some loose change in the wishing pond. Let's hope it works for us," said Nieman.

"But even if he agrees to release the land, he might come up with some hard terms. Remember, he's had some paralegal training," said Missy.

"You mean like he might want half the profits."

"No, other things—he isn't interested in money. But speaking of money, this job's starting to take all my time, and who's paying me?"

"I'll pay you in old wines and kisses."

"Hard to pay bills with that, mister, but that does remind me of the job offer."

"Yeah, I'd like to know about that."

"He offered me a job to head up regional legal affairs for the Midwest office out of Indianapolis." She explained the offer. "They'd even maintain an office for me in Indy, and I'd just go when needed."

"A hell of a deal." Nieman suddenly showed concern. "You seriously thinking about taking it?"

"You know, a girl has to follow her ambitions sometimes." She smirked. "Just kidding. He said I could still maintain my practice here. I mean, what would I do without all the Swan's legal problems you'd get yourself into?"

"Probably, but I wouldn't have anymore emotional problems either." He glanced around to see an empty lobby, pulled her to him, and kissed her.

"What do we do now, innkeeper?"

"Ah, with the hotel?" He asked. "I guess we just have to wait for a decision from Indian country."

"That answer will do for now. Have to run. I still have a whole day of clients. See you later."

Chapter 53

A Nod—with Conditions

It was a worrisome morning for the Swan manager. Only two days after Missy returned from Atlanta, Faith called to say she was bringing Indian Joe to the hotel. "He's ready to talk."

She said he had spent the morning going through the contents of the box sent from Louisville and then meditating again out in the fields in the afternoon. She told Nieman he kept staring at each piece, especially the headdress.

"It was like he was mesmerized by everything." "He just fondled the tribal relics. But he did say—more than once—that it is time. I asked if that meant time to talk about the land at the Swan, and he nodded but insisted that Missy be there too at any meeting."

Nieman stroked his chin, popped a lemon drop in his mouth, and paced back and forth across the lobby for what seemed to him an eternity. The few guests loitering there watched him, likely wondering what was going to happen, when the front door flew open.

Faith and Missy each had an arm of a stern-faced Indian Joe as they led him across the lobby. A startled Nieman gaped at the Indian, no longer in tattered jeans and a porkpie hat. He stood resplendent in the restored headdress, which nearly reached the floor, and he donned a pair of tribal armlets, along with the rawhide leg wrappings and the chest plate ornamented with pearls, shells, eagle talons, and colorful seed pods, all cleaned and polished.

"Lee," said a smiling Missy, with a stage bow and sweeping hand gesture, "let us introduce you to our friend, Mr. Tom Eagleman, He of the Long Feather, who has been so gracious as to share with us his satisfaction in your recapturing his tribal legacy."

Nieman, who seldom lacked words, was speechless for a few awkward moments.

"Ah, Mr. Eagleman," he finally managed, "I am so very proud of sharing in your pleasure. And for the long-ago owners of this establishment, I am happy to pass on an apology for past slights. I hope you and I can be friends."

"Perhaps," said the aged Indian, standing erect, arms folded, shoulders back. "But I do want to thank you deeply for restoring my tribe's lost honor. Wearing all this is a humbling experience, since it was never mine but my grandfather's. He finally spoke to me in a spirit vision as I meditated. So I wear it in tribute to him and all my ancestors."

He continued as everyone in the lobby looked on. "Yes, I will be your friend and a special friend of Miss Landrew, who has a true understanding of my delicate position here. I find myself arranging the future of land that was never mine but the whole tribal family's. But I do it for those who once stewarded the land and lived and caught game there, and who were eventually evicted from the same land those many years ago."

He held up a sheath of papers he'd been holding under his arm.

"Unlike treaties of the past between my tribe and the white people, this document that your friend and I have drawn up holds nothing that would cause you any concern. Oh, no, my young friend," he said, smiling, "this Indian hasn't taken a page from the white man's treachery in past treaties. Certainly you won't find any hidden clauses that could cause problems, only a few modest considerations."

"I don't expect any hidden small print or double-talk," said Nieman, fingers crossed behind him. "I'm sure any provision our friend here proposes has been sincerely considered with no ambiguities. I have no doubts about his integrity. As far as I'm concerned, He of the Long Feather is a straight shooter."

"Oh, you can say that again, Mr. Nieman," Faith said. "Why, down at the creek just yesterday, our friend was showing me how to use a slingshot, and he plunked a black bird out of the sky as we stood there."

"Aha," Eagleman said. "Like many things in life, Miss Quinton, it's only a matter of perception. A half dozen or so birds like that can make a good meal. You see starlings; I see baked squab, maybe with mushroom sauce added."

After sharing in the humor, Nieman broke in. "To get back on point, Mr. Eagleman, can we agree that our problem here has been resolved, with honor to your tribe?"

"It has been, but only because I haven't long to live and I realize that when I'm gone the world will have no memory of my forefathers and our tribe's place in the world. Paramount in our agreement, as Miss Landrew will explain, is keeping that memory alive forever."

Chapter 54

Indian Terms

"How exactly would that be accomplished?" a nervous Nieman asked while fearing the answer he'd get.

"I will let Miss Landrew explain all the terms we've discussed, but my most heartfelt desire is to see a permanent memorial erected here on our original campgrounds, one that boldly commemorates our heritage and our code of trust and fairness."

There was a moment of silence. *My god*, Nieman thought. *He wants a pyramid!*

"We're talking a plaque on a rock, Lee," Missy said in his ear, sensing his worry.

"Well, I see no problem with that," said a relieved Nieman, but deep down knowing there'd be more to any peace pact with this crafty Native American.

Almost on cue, Eagleman spoke. "Now, of course, there are a few other provisions we're considering. I'll let Miss Landrew spell them out for you in contract language."

"Based on your many years of dealing with others, I'm sure whatever you ask for will be reasonable," Nieman said.

"Thank you for your faith in my judgement, but I must caution you on a point. It is true that I have lived an exceptionally long life, but that doesn't automatically assure I've understood everything."

He continued. "Despite the many imponderables life holds, I've found wisdom can be a playful mistress. It is true that the older I become, the more I know, but at the same time, the more I find that I do not know or understand."

"Very insightful Mr. Eagleman," said Nieman, wondering where this conversation was going.

"I might add," the Indian said, "the certainty of the future is always a fickle matter too. I do hope that after I'm gone you'll still maintain the moral spirit of your great General Grant in running your business. I admire the man."

Nieman nodded.

"If you remember your nation's history, you know that when the general became president, he strongly urged fairness in treatment of the defeated Confederates and, by the same principle, supported humane and fair treatment of Native Americans in the West, while others were thoughtless of their suffering in defeat."

"I probably missed the chapter on Grant in history class," said Nieman.

"My young friend, your General Grant is often misjudged."

"Apparently so. I always had the impression he was just a bad president."

"Not so much to Indians at the time. In his administration a plan called 'The Great Peace Policy' was proposed, to enforce fairness to Indian tribes. He even felt Indians should have citizenship in time."

"Really?"

"Oh yes. He has been unappreciated as a president, but to the Indians at the time, he was—how do you say it?—a stand-up guy in the way he dealt with others, even his enemies. I must urge you also to treat your hotel patrons and those with whom you will do business equally and with fairness and respect."

"We plan to conduct our business with that in mind."

"Excellent," the Indian responded. "But I want that in writing too. White men have always wanted more and have always broken peace treaties with betrayals. Here, I ask little while I'm giving much."

Missy, knowing that clients were waiting in her office, broke in. "We understand your concerns and intend to strictly follow the terms of our agreement. But I have to run now. You and I can look over the terms this afternoon at the gazebo, and you can sign the release."

"If Mr. Nieman signs first," said Indian Joe.

"Of course. Now would you like a room for tonight?"

"No, thank you. The outdoors is my element, as you know." Still wearing the long, full-feathered headdress, he walked out into the cool autumn morning, passers-by likely wondering if the hotel was hosting a pre-holiday Halloween costume party.

Chapter 55

Loaded Peace Treaty

Later, in Nieman's office Missy went over the pages of notes she'd taken after parlaying with Indian Joe most of the day.

"He sure looked magnificent in that headdress," said Nieman. "Just like a real Indian chief would look, like those old pictures of Sitting Bull and Chief Joseph. I just kept thinking about all the history involved."

"I did too. I never knew until Faith told me that the tribe originally had their encampment here by the hotel. The town pushed them out to the country after that." She looked up from her notes. "These past two months have been a real adventure, haven't they?"

"Yes, but let's get to it. I almost hate to ask what else he wants before he signs the release."

"Don't look so grim. It's not all that bad."

"Right. C'mon, let me have it."

"Well, the memorial he mentioned has to be noticeable: big and outside on the lawn. He wanted it in polished marble with a silver plaque on it about the tribe's history ... and ten feet tall."

"Good grief. Even Columbus didn't get one that big, and he discovered America."

"But he wasn't our friend. Anyway, I got him down to a six-foot Indiana boulder with a bronze plaque. I told him marble would probably have to come from another state."

"Okay. What else does he want? This is getting ridiculous," Nieman asked.

"I think this one is pretty funny. He wants you to get rid of that wooden cigar store Indian in the lobby."

"What? Why? It's a neat curiosity for visitors to see."

"He says tobacco wasn't native to America. It was planted here by white Colonials just to make money. Anyway, he thinks we shouldn't be displaying something like smoking that's bad for your health."

"Oh, God. Okay. We can put it in storage. What's the next surprise?"

"He wants to be able to stay at the Swan indefinitely. And because he can't easily live off the land around here, he's asking for one meal a day from the hotel kitchen."

"Holy cow! This is getting expensive."

"Lee, the man is ninety-five years old. How many meals does he have left?"

"Okay, okay." He rubbed his forehead. "I feel a headache coming on. What else?"

"He wants that old, broken-down convertible in the carriage house garage."

"Why? It's worthless. Doesn't even run."

"He said Boney told him he'd help him fix it up, so he could drive it in local parades. He'll put a banner on it about supporting Indian charities. "

"What'd you tell him?"

"I said okay, but he'd have to put another flag or banner on it advertising the Swan."

"Oh, what the hell. I don't care. It won't cost us anything."

"No, but the next thing might."

"I'm afraid to ask what it is. Boy, this Indian should have been a Teamster negotiator. He wants everything. Well, lay it on me."

"Now remember, this is the last thing on the list, Lee"

"Right. I won't bet on it."

"Well, he, ah, wants a tiny piece of the action, like 3 percent of our gross revenues."

"What! Are you kidding? I'm not doing that. We'll be lucky to make 3 percent net profit off the gross. No way."

"I told him no too, and I got him to agree to 1 percent of our net profit. And I explained there isn't apt to be any for a long time. Okay?" Missy said.

"Not really," Nieman said.

"C'mon, Lee; it's not for him. It's for the United Indian Charities."

"What's that?"

"It's a nonprofit that helps feed Indian families that are too poor to buy enough food and don't get much government assistance."

Nieman grabbed his forehead for a moment. "I'm beginning to think I shouldn't have dreamed this up in the first place. Okay, but make it a half percent. Now, that's the end, right?"

"Well," she said, looking down at her notes, "I did forget one thing, but it won't cost you any money."

"I bet. What now?"

"He wants a provision that bars us from ever turning the Swan into a casino."

"That's an easy yes," Nieman said." We aren't planning to do that anyway—are we?"

"No, but remember the place is on Native American land, so we could."

"Actually, I hadn't thought about it." He paused and stroked his chin. "Casino gambling is legal in Indiana now, isn't it?"

"Yes, so you have to give him credit for thinking of it," Missy said.

"So, if we did that he'd probably want 10 percent for the Indian charity. Speaking of Indians, where's our friend now?"

"Outside, setting up his tent for the night, I suppose."

"Tent?"

"Remember, he doesn't like beds with mattresses. Too soft."

"Not me," said Nieman. "I gotta get up early tomorrow and call everybody who's in on this. A soft bed sounds great to me."

"I'm ready to call it a day too," she said as they stood to leave.

"You know," said Nieman, putting his arms around her and pulling her close, "after all we've been through, we really should have a few drinks over this tomorrow—and celebrate."

"Oh, I think there'll be more than celebrating going on." They kissed, and she left grinning, leaving the Swan's soon-to-be owner wondering what that puzzling grin meant.

Chapter 56

A Powwow for All

Nieman got out of bed before sunrise. He had to phone the home office to turn in his resignation and announce he was finally ready for a closing on the Swan.

He'd have to pass on the good news to the mayor and sit down with Curly and Boney to explain the new agreement and how their investments, small as they were, would help him come up with the down payment, enhanced with proceeds from wine auctions and the liberation of "hidden value" from several antiques stored in the old ballroom.

Between calls, he walked back to the kitchen for another cup of coffee and noticed no one seemed to be in the lobby, or anywhere for that matter. And he couldn't find Boney, who was always on the job. It was all too quiet. Slowly he became aware he was hearing more noise from outside than inside, and he took a look out the kitchen window.

People were milling around the hotel grounds. He spotted a group of children running and skipping toward the back of the hotel property. From where he stood, he couldn't see where they were headed, but they weren't stopping at the Grant Wishing Pond, where kids and tourists usually went when they came to town. He headed outside and almost ran into Boney, who was running up the steps to the front door.

"Boss, uh, we havin' some kind of celebration or, or somethin'? I been rakin' leaves, and people started showing up ever'where."

"Wish I knew what's going on too, Boney."

Nearby, a large TV van carrying a rooftop antenna abruptly pulled over the curb and sidewalk and up on the lawn, the driver trying his best not to run over anyone. Nieman handed Boney his cup of coffee and ran to the driver's window. "Hey, you can't pull up on this lawn, buddy. Where you going? What's the rush?"

"I'm not sure, mister. I was just told to come down here and let our anchor get some footage of that Indian and his teepee. I'll go around back. Sorry about the grass."

The van backed into the street, leaving Nieman muttering to himself, "Teepee? Indian?" He turned to Boney. "Where's Missy? I bet she knows what's up."

"Must be back there, where everybody's headed. I'm going too."

Nieman watched Boney scramble across the lawn and then spotted Missy coming toward him through a tangle of people by the wishing pond.

"What the hell's going on?" he shouted.

"Just calm down now, Lee," she said as she reached the veranda. "Isn't it wonderful what Indian Joe is doing for us ... and that teepee. This is hysterical." She wagged her finger toward the back of the hotel grounds.

"Hysterical? I guess, but what's this teepee business? I thought ..."

He stepped out farther on the grass and followed her gaze.

Chapter 57

Media Frenzy

"**What?** Is this a joke?" Nieman's jaw dropped. There it was, rising from the swale behind the carriage house. He could only see the top of what was obviously a canvas teepee, the conical tip reaching nearly to the Swan's second floor, a thin ribbon of white smoke rising from an opening at the top. He grabbed Missy's hand, and they both followed the crowd.

"This'll ruin us. You didn't tell me he was going to camp out like this ... in a teepee. We can't have that."

Now he could see Indian Joe, wearing the headdress, standing in front of the teepee, and talking to a man with a microphone.

"I didn't think you'd approve. But remember, Lee; we did agree to let him stay *at* the hotel. Doesn't matter whether that's outside or inside. Besides, think about it: no changing of his sheets, no room to clean, no need for room service."

"But this is ridiculous. We'll look like fools. And that thing probably violates all the city's zoning codes. What were you thinking?" He pressed a fist against his forehead as they watched the scene.

"Don't worry," she said. "I talked to the mayor; he's here in the crowd, and he's exuberant about it and said they'll write a zoning variance for us."

A young woman holding a small note pad and tape recorder jumped from a panel truck of an Indianapolis TV station and rushed up to them.

"You the hotel manager?"

Nieman nodded.

"I wonder if you could comment on all this activity being caused by a Native American from Indianapolis? We've heard he's named Long Feather and is the last of a tribe that lived here a long time ago." She switched on her tape recorder and stuck it in his face.

"Well, ah ... I, ah ... yes, of course, it's a long story ... but, ah, a long time ago ..."

Missy chuckled. She had no doubt Nieman was enjoying the moment, even if he didn't show it as he went on with the Chikopik story. She moved a few feet away and pressed through a knot of wide-eyed spectators watching the Indian now deep in an interview with another news reporter.

Other TV and print reporters were waiting their turn, and photographers were clicking away at what would likely be their stations' lead story on the evening news and a front-page feature for the print media who'd shown up for the occasion.

An Indy video photographer asked Indian Joe to bring his drum out of the teepee and pose with it for still shots. He was the star attraction as he went on giving all comers sound bites.

All tape recorder red lights came on when he talked about the "old days" when "white men and government officials treated Native Americans with no respect. We and our Western brothers were cheated out of our lands and pushed out to land that was worthless. Whites saw us—and many still see us—as just laggards and worthless, emotionless dummies and drunks."

One reporter asked, "Mr. Long Feather, we're told you're an admirer of Ulysses S. Grant. Why is that?"

"In those long-ago years," he said, standing erect with his arms crossed over his chest, "many Native Americans learned to look fondly on the general because he respected minorities. He was the first Union general to use African American troops in the Civil War, and he advocated fairness in dealing with Indians in the West. He even proposed a national Indian Peace Plan, and when he was president …" Long after most reporters had stopped taking notes, he went on and on.

Photographers pressed Long Feather to pose by the wishing pond as he was being interviewed. He obliged and, with a faint smile and careful not to drag the trailing headdress feathers on the ground as he walked, strode to the pond, followed by an eager gaggle of reporters and photographers.

Video cameras lit up, and still photographers clicked away. One news reporter asked if he once hunted game in the area.

The Indian said, "Of course. We all did to help feed our tribe. You're not a hunter, I take it?" he asked the reporter, surprised to be questioned.

"No, but how'd you know that?"

"Being a reporter, you were probably an English major in college? Right?"

"Yes, but so what?"

"Hunting is a quiet venture, young man. English majors talk too much."

Everyone around him, taken off guard by the humor, suddenly roared with laughter, even the reporter who was the butt of the Indian's remark.

"I'm told that kids make wishes at the pond," said one late-arriving radio personality. "Could I ask, in your opinion, what would General Grant likely ask for if he were here today by the pond?"

The Indian paused for a moment and then straightened, shoulders back, and responded. "I believe he would probably say it's time for all of us, black, white, red, Latino, and Asian, rich and poor, to understand each other and treat each other fairly before my native country fractures."

The crowd clapped and murmured approval.

"Perceptions, my friends, are increasingly too often replacing truth in our nation."

"Thank you, Chief," said the newsman. He put down his microphone and motioned to his cameraman to shut down while he chatted with a fellow Indianapolis anchor. Nieman overheard him whisper, "Boy, how'd this guy get so smart? Really articulate—for an Indian."

Nieman listened for a few more minutes and then turned to leave but found a clearly excited Mayor Gomia walking toward him.

"Son, you've done it now," he said with his toothy grin. "You've put us on the map with this Indian. I knew I was putting my money on the right horse. Grantville's going to be a destination city, and what better way to get our new name out there. We couldn't have bought publicity like this."

Embarrassed, knowing Missy was behind all the hubbub, Nieman thanked the mayor and decided to go back to his office to escape anymore misplaced plaudits or on-camera interviews. He grabbed Handley's arm and yelled at Boney to follow him to the Swan's veranda.

"If you're asked by the media for an interview, be sure to mention that we're planning on restoring the place and we'll have a grand opening in a few months. We might even have a few rooms with bathrooms by then." He gave a thumbs-up, and they both did the same.

Chapter 58

In-House Toast

"Sir," said Handley, leaning close to Nieman so he wouldn't be heard by the sudden collection of people on the veranda, "don't you think it's about time to celebrate? Perhaps we could toast the occasion by opening a few of those vintage wines."

"Well, okay, Curly, but just take a couple of the old ones—not the best ones, though—but be sure to save the bottles. We can display them to remember the origins of the new Silver Swan Inn."

Handley headed to the front desk counter, where he had stowed two of the bottles retrieved from underground.

"It is time for a celebration," Nieman said to the employees mingling on the veranda. "And look who's joining us."

Faith Quinton had made her way through the crowd, camera in hand. "No one called me," she said to Nieman.

"Sorry, Faith. I didn't know all this was going to happen."

"Oh, I know, but the town historian can't miss out on a singular event like this. It's like the old days, when all the VIPs stayed here."

Suddenly she spotted the Swan's maintenance man. But Boney had already seen her and was backing out of the knot of employees.

"Why, Mr. Pieratt, I'm so glad to see you again. You're not leaving, are you?"

He turned, offering a smile of defeat.

Bottles in hand, Handley returned in time to see Pieratt's discomfort. He broke in, gesturing to Faith, Boney, and Nieman. "People, just follow me to the barroom for a toast. I believe this might be the appropriate time for a toast." He held the two green, handblown glass bottles aloft with one hand and a corkscrew in other.

"I will propose a toast to General Grant ... and to our Native American here, who the general never met but would have understood ... and to the general's attitude of respect for all people. I think he would have approved of even such a small gesture."

"He most certainly would have," said Faith. "If he could be here today at the wishing pond, he very likely would wish for just that."

"Anyone care to join me for a historic decanting?" asked Handley as he turned toward the Swan's dining room, where Indiana's elite once cavorted.

Faith beckoned again to Pieratt. "Now you wouldn't mind taking me along to the toasting, dear man, would you?" She hooked her arm in his. "It's been such a long time since you've been out at my place. It looks like it'd be a good weekend for enjoying the out-of-doors in the country—and you haven't seen my new addition. Of course it isn't quite finished yet, but ..."

"Well, ma'am, I, uh, I really am, ah ... kind of busy."

"Come on, now, you sweet man; let's go with Mr. Handley and join in the toast. We can talk about my addition later, or not."

"Well, ah ...

"Certainly you want to join us, dear boy," she said, pulling him along, heading to the dining room.

Nieman and Missy laughed but then were amazed and in disbelief when they saw Sylvia Norton step out of her chauffeured car at the curb and walk up to the hotel.

All heads turned as she yelled, "Yoo hoo, Mr. Handley."

Handley had just stepped into the lobby and turned around as she started up the steps, one hand on the hand rail, the other gripping a white, loose-woven shawl around her shoulders.

"Why, Miss Norton, so glad you've come." He put the wines down on a small serving table, took her hand in one of his, and patted it with the other. "It's been so long since we've seen you."

"You know, Charles, you are the only real gentleman at this establishment and the only one around here who appreciates the subtleties of fine living. You do understand me, don't you, dear man?"

Handley smiled eagerly as he continued to hold her hand. "Of course, madam."

"Now, since I've decided these people can go ahead and restore my family's legacy, I may as well enjoy the old place one last time, before they turn it into a Motel 6 with a doughnut vending machine."

"Quite so, madam." Handley brought her hand up and kissed it as onlookers murmured approval. "We're about to take part in a small afternoon soiree, so to speak, to mark the beginning of the Silver Swan's new future. Certainly you'll join us?"

"Oh, I might be tempted, if you would escort me and I could have a glass of sherry, if you have any."

"*Après vous*, dear lady." A beaming Handley bowed slightly and swept his hand toward the lobby as he opened the door for her. "Of course we have sherry, the best, straight from Spain and quite old. Madam is certain to enjoy it."

"Oh, you are such an actor, Charles." She took his arm, and he grabbed the two bottles off the table. The group began moving into the lobby, headed for the dining room, Handley singing an old British drinking song and hoisting the bottles of wine in the air.

Enjoying the scene, Nieman and Missy followed the others as they caught the brassy sound of the high school marching band moving toward the hotel, playing "Back Home Again in Indiana."

The cheerleaders gyrated around with a cheer: "Grantville, Grantville is our new name, but our Plainview spirit's still the same."

The two stood at the door for a few minutes, hand in hand, listening to the music.

"You know, I can't believe I left the big city to find this kind of happiness in a town so small that no one would even stop here unless they had a flat tire," said Nieman.

"Or if they fell in love with someone here."

"Good point, counselor." They looked deep into each other's eyes, kissed, and headed to what was once the preferred dining spot for the Midwest's rich and famous and those who wanted to be.

Epilogue

Lee Nieman and Missy Landrew were married a couple of months later in a ceremony in the Swan's fourth-floor Norton Family Ballroom, where restoration work was still in progress. The staff still managed to decorate it for the occasion. They even used the contractor's ladders and scaffolding to hang banners and white-and-blue crepe paper around the large room and a canopy over the ceremonial area.

Boney Pieratt and Faith Quinton did not marry, but Boney did volunteer occasionally to lug a few more rocks up the banks of Chikopik Creek to help her complete her addition.

Sylvia Norton was seen occasionally with Curly Handley at local social occasions, though, apparently, they never became more than just close friends. Townspeople used the term *escort* when referring to Handley's role with her.

As far as is known, Sylvia never told Curly or anyone else why she relinquished her small stake in the hotel, and true to her word, Faith never revealed the secret. But she told close friends that in a future, second edition of her book on local history, she would reveal "some delicious family secrets," secrets she alone possessed of "certain" leading families of the community.

Nieman and the other investors had to wait for well over a year before the hotel showed any meaningful profits. Even then the costs of installing both men's and women's bath accommodations kept any distribution of net revenues at a minimum for another year or so. No one complained about that, not even the mayor.

The Swan's maintenance man and night auditor both stayed on the job for years to come. Boney, having attended some trade schools and finally learned the fine arts of welding and plumbing and how to fix broken toilets.

Missy Landrew-Nieman continued to run her law practice and eventually ran for city council, winning a seat. She did finally accept the part-time legal position with the Swinton Corporation, only finding it necessary to travel to her Indianapolis office a time or two each month.

The restored Swan eventually attracted a steady flow of visitors, overnight guests often coming just to see the oldest inn in the Hoosier State and enjoy the history and antiques of the place, not to mention the reputed ghost.

Mike Cole, whom Nieman replaced as Swan manager, called not long after the Nieman group bought the property and joined the others in making an investment. Nieman readily gave him credit—via his cryptic reminder note—for the idea of using the "hidden value" in some of the Swan's antiques to help finance hotel operations. Cole admitted he'd quit without notice for fear the corporation wouldn't appreciate his technique for fleshing out the monthly income reports.

By the time the Swan began generating net income, Nieman, with Missy's help, had sold off about a fourth of the Swan's excess antiques to beef up operating income and help pay for some of the restoration. But many of the authentic pieces were rearranged for easier viewing by visitors.

The antique music box on the second floor, along with two Chippendale couches and some other notable vintage pieces, were moved to the lobby so visitors who came just for the history of the Swan could get a feel for it upon entering.

The town of Grantville did not quite become, as Mayor Gomia predicted, a major "destination city," but with boosted visitor traffic to the Swan, the city did continue to grow and become a notable Indiana historic landmark once again.

Indian Joe, a.k.a. Tom Eagleman, a.k.a. He of the Long Feather, and his teepee had a lot to do with that, drawing the curious from a wide area of the Midwest and becoming a landmark on his own. When he died, his obituary was carried in many large daily papers, and representatives from several other states' Indian tribes showed up to honor a peer whose cause championed understanding for all ethnic groups. On the Swan's lawn, his tombstone inscription read: "A warrior who long sought to restore respect for Native Americans."

Nearby, the history of the Chikopik tribe remained engraved on a plaque on a huge boulder. Visitors almost always made it a point to see the tombstone and boulder as they strolled over the tribe's long-ago campgrounds after lunch or dinner, or after frolicking in the Norton Family Ballroom.

As this epilogue was written, the ghost of Grant's one-time nubile playmate was never seen again, or at the least was never reported being seen. But, after all, the restored Silver Swan Inn's new history was only just beginning.

The End

www.ingramcontent.com/pod-product-compliance
Lightning Source LLC
LaVergne TN
LVHW091544060526
838200LV00036B/695